SAN JOAQUIN VALLEY LIBRARY SYSTEM
1039966690

West of Nowhere

Other Five Star Titles
by Alan LeMay:

Spanish Crossing (1998)
The Bells of San Juan (2001)

West of Nowhere

WESTERN STORIES

ALAN LeMAY

Five Star • Waterville, Maine

This collection is a work of fiction. Names, characters, places, and incidents are either the product of the author's imagination, or, if real, used fictitiously.

Five Star First Edition Western Series.

Published in 2002 in conjunction with Golden West Literary Agency.

Cover design by Thorndike Press Staff.

Set in 11 pt. Plantin.

Printed in the United States on permanent paper.

Library of Congress Cataloging-in-Publication Data

LeMay, Alan, 1899–1964.
West of Nowhere : western stories / by Alan LeMay.
p. cm.—(Five Star first edition western series)
ISBN 0-7862-3530-6 (hc : alk. paper)
1. Western stories. I. Title. II. Series.
PS3523.E513 W47 2002
813′.52—dc21 2002276824

Table of Contents

Foreword

In the dusky prairie skies west of nowhere Alan LeMay, my father, was putting the finishing touches on a long day of solo flying. The year was 1938, and the Kansas plains had few towns or highways to guide an amateur pilot. The sun was setting in his eyes, which he figured was a good thing since his dead-reckoning navigation was intended to take him back to California. As it grew dark, he saw in the distance the welcome sight of lights marking the boundaries of the dirt-strip airfield that was today's destination. All was well. Another triumph of man over crosswind.

But then the lights went out. The field that had been so clearly outlined in the distance disappeared. The sun was gone—there was no moon—the high overcast blanketed the stars, and the lonely prairie ate the airfield. As he drew near the vanished target, a line of widely spaced red lights appeared, and off to the side was a dim glow from the window of the fixed-base operations shack. Dad buzzed it, revving the tired engine as a signal to get the lights on for a landing. No response. He circled back, and, after a lot more engine signaling, the door opened and a man stood in the dim splash of light, waving. One more pass and the man went back inside. But still no field lights.

So Dad lined up on the red lights, eased the throttle back, and glided in to the field he could not see. The plane settled down until the red lights flashed past close below on one side. He pulled the stick back, keeping the plane just above the level of the lights, raising the nose to stall the taildragger into a three-point landing. But the plane did not touch down. There was a sickening several seconds of free fall, followed by the major crunch that comes from stalling thirty feet too high.

Miraculously the landing gear survived. The lights had not been at runway level, they were on the tops of the power poles that seemed always to appear near short airstrips. So in the appropriate mood of one who has just nearly killed himself, Dad stormed into the operations shack to ask why they couldn't spare ten minutes of power for the welcome lights.

"I'll bet you make a living straightening bent airplanes."

"Why, you bend yours? I didn't think your landing was that noisy. All four bounces sounded right side up."

"Well, I guess I could do that blindfolded, because that's what it's like out there. What's the deal here, incoming pilots have to pay in advance for a little electricity? You don't put out much of a welcome mat."

"Sorry about the misunderstanding. A fella just left on a night flight to Dallas. You probably saw the field lights when he took off. Then, when you buzzed us, we thought it was him, waving good bye. Anyways, good thing you didn't take those red lights as runway center line, that could have left us without power for our coffee pot."

Dad's cross-country solo, Boston to San Diego, would be routine today. But in a fabric-covered Tailorcraft, lacking decent weather reports and carrying minimal navigation equipment, it was a challenge. He had few hours in the air, but he was getting experience the way he liked it: fast and first-hand. He was thinking about writing some flying stories, but first he had to do it himself.

He mostly wrote Westerns because they dealt with people, places, and a way of life that he knew and loved. He knew horses because he spent a lot of time with them. He rode them in the heat of the Carrizo desert, rounding up wild horses. He rode them in polo matches, wearing out a half dozen horses a game. He rode them on Sunday morning paper chases with us kids. He rode them at night in freezing rain when his herd of pregnant whitefaces needed a cowboy midwife. He owned a horse that he could talk to, and one that would bite him if he turned his back. When he wrote of the jarring wake-up call a bronc' gives his rider to start the day, the description rings true because he always topped off his own bronc's.

And it was that way with the flying: first the experience, then the writing. Connoisseurs of Westerns claim that the term Western denotes an action style with heroes winning out over villains, and covers a lot more than just the horse-borne era in the grandeur of the American West. So the title piece of this collection happens to be about airplanes and pilots, rather than horses and cowboys, but I would still call it a Western. And you can be sure that the background is authentic and based on the author's first-hand experience, because it is by Alan LeMay.

Dan LeMay
Fallbrook, California

Death Rides the Trionte

I

"BACK FROM THE DEAD"

Buck Williams's bar echoed to the shouting and laughter of a dozen hard-eyed men who gathered about Wade Jeffries. They had returned from an expedition that had ended entirely to the satisfaction of Jeffries.

A range king, immaculate in expensive soft-brimmed Stetson, silk shirt, and doeskin chaps and vest, he smiled as he touched his thin lips with a small glass. It was a mirthless smile, a cold, emotionless widening of the lips. It was a smile that might have been painted beneath frowning eyes on the mouth of a statue.

"Yore enemies don't seem to last long, Wade," gloated Lin Walters, a tall, lanky gunny with a huge nose and small, shifty eyes. "That's the last we'll see o' Dale Manley unless his ghost gits up and walks. He died a lot easier'n that dog o' his'n. I had to shoot the danged brute four times before it let loose o' my leg."

Gar Dixon, a heavy, powerful man with a shock of red hair and a livid scar running from forehead to chin, glanced about him. "Yuh ought to buckle up that lip o' yore'n, Lin," he growled. "We ain't advertisin' what we done today."

"We're all friends here," retorted the tall gunman, "and anything goes. Besides, yuh know it wasn't us that wiped out Dale Manley. Oh, no! It was that masked outfit o' rannies that stuck up the stage last week, and run off them three-year-olds that Wade had over on the branch. We got a deputy sheriff with us, so what the hell?"

A grim, black-eyed man, with a silver star glittering on his cowhide vest, nodded. "I figger the law wanted Dale Manley," he remarked with a ghost of a smile. "He was shot while tryin' to escape. It's an old Spanish custom."

Jeffries sipped the liquor in the thin glass. His attitude was one of power and extreme satisfaction—satisfaction with himself, satisfaction with the world. The last of his enemies had gone down in a red ruin. Dale Manley, who had blocked his plan for taking over the entire Trionte Valley that lay like a green gem between two ranges of smoky hills, with its miles of smooth, grass-covered prairie and low, lush hay land, was gone forever.

A cattle king and a cold, ambitious killer was Wade Jeffries. He rode over men as he rode over the great range. Whoever should stand in his way must die. Wade Jeffries was the All Highest of the Trionte. His will was the law.

First had gone Bliss Hathaway. Next Dan Morgan, a gentleman who had called everyone his friend, had died face downward in a fire. Dale Manley had followed today. There were lesser ones, such as Bart Connel and Jim Lessert of the Cross C, but they did not count.

Sometimes there had been a woman at stake, for Jeffries was a noted squire of dames. The crime of Dale Manley had been two-fold. He had owned the Flying Q, and Stella Carter had smiled upon him, instead of upon Wade Jeffries.

"So far," Gar Dixon threw out viciously, "there ain't nobody got the best o' Wade except them masked *hombres* that held up the stage last week and took the payroll. Who do yuh suppose they are, anyway? Where do they come from?"

"From hell!" snapped Jeffries as he crashed the glass down on the bar. "And they're goin' back, if it's my last act. I'll hound 'em. . . ."

He stopped speaking, stared at a man who had entered silently and now stood motionless in the doorway. A bloody bandage was tied about his head, and his face was white as the pallor of the grave. He stood with folded arms and did not speak.

"Dale Manley!" gasped the cattle king.

All eyes followed his, and silently the wide-eyed men stared at this man who they had left for dead on the grass-covered slope of the Flying Q. So complete was the silence that the ticking of the old Seth Thomas clock over the bar was clearly audible.

Gar Dixon began swearing softly—hoarse, violent oaths that seemed to come from deep down in his throat.

The young man in the doorway spoke between tense, drawn lips. "I followed yuh, Wade Jeffries. Yuh and yore rotten gunnies. I know who yuh are. I know every one of yuh. Let's have it out right now, Jeffries. That's what I come for. Go for yore gun. Let's see what yuh can do to a man with yore hired killers keepin' out of it. Have yuh got the nerve to shoot it out with me?"

The cattle king licked his dry lips. His hands remained conspicuously away from the holster that swung low against his thigh. He shot a swift glance at Gar Dixon, who was his fastest gunman, and who drew fighting wages the year around.

Dixon's brows narrowed as he stared at Dale Manley. Then his hand shot down, and his gun flashed in the lamp-light.

Manley half turned. A streak of flame stabbed out from under his arm, and the crash of a .44 shattered the stillness.

Dixon's knees buckled. The gun dropped from his hand, and he sank to the floor.

Manley dropped flat as Jeffries's men came to life. Flaming guns appeared in their hands. Again a .44 roared. The big lamp careened crazily and crashed to the floor in a stream of burning oil that splashed out over the men. Lin Walters screamed as his clothing burst into flames.

Manley backed out of the doorway into the darkness. He staggered as he made his way to the hitch rack in front of the saloon. A stream of warm blood trickled down from underneath a bandage. The lights in the little street seemed to be waving up and down and around in incomplete circles.

A horse loomed before him. Mechanically he loosed the two half-hitches that tied it, and climbed into the saddle. With the touch of a spur it leaped forward into the street. A bullet whipped by him, and then another. He lay close to the horse's back and wondered how he might escape the horde that would come pounding on his trail. Then he questioned if he really wanted to escape, or if he should turn and see how many of Wade Jeffries's killers he could stop before a bullet brought him face to face with the long trail.

The last light of the little town slipped by, and he was out on the prairie headed straight for a great star that hung low in the western sky. He wondered about that star. Night after night he had watched it, and had noticed how much brighter it was than its fellows.

Again and again he heard the grim *whine* of bullets. Turning weakly, he could see the hazy outline of a dozen mounted men following in the darkness. He knew Jeffries's men were well mounted, and that he could not escape from them on the little pinto. Then he realized he was not on the pinto. That head, with ears erect, the easy stride that ate up the miles tirelessly, could belong to but one animal on the Trionte. By mistake he had taken the Thoroughbred bay gelding for which Wade Jeffries had paid five thousand dollars. Manley grinned to himself and sat straighter in the saddle. By the irony of fate he was escaping on the horse of his enemy—the only horse that could outrun the mounts of the angry men behind.

The star loomed big and bright ahead. Manley thought he must be gaining on it, for it seemed bigger than a moment before. He began to laugh and shout hysterically. He emptied his gun into the air.

Wade Jeffries! Hang Wade Jeffries! What cared Dale Manley for the cattle king who had hounded him from his home? Here was night and a star. A magnificent horse strained beneath him. A cool wind blew against his face, drying the blood that still trickled out from under the red bandage.

He turned and jeered at the men behind, and there was no answer. Already he had outdistanced them. Straight toward the hills the gelding dashed. Why the hills? Why not? Manley did not care where the sweating, lathering, dashing animal took him. Why should he?

The star was jumping crazily about in the heavens. The dark outline of the hills weaved in a weird and strange motion like a Gargantuan dance of giant things that were beyond the knowledge of men.

Manley shouted again. What cared he? Let all creation dance. Let the hills tumble down over the earth. Let them bury him and Wade Jeffries beneath the ruin of the world and he would be content.

Weakness assailed him, and he sank forward in the saddle, gripping the horn with both hands. He knew the horse was covered with foam and was panting for breath, and that its red nostrils were dilated to the utmost with the killing pace. Slowly he spoke the quiet words that he had often used to soothe cattle at night. He found the reins and pulled gently. The hills seemed to leap forward, and the next moment he was among them.

Gradually the pace slackened, and the heaving animal came to a stop.

Manley remained a moment with the stars whirling above him, and then fell gently from the saddle. He did not hear voices that came out of the night. He did not feel the hands that lifted him. He did not know when he was placed in a horse litter made from two saplings and a blanket. He did not know when they stopped at a little cabin hidden away among a thick growth of spruce in the fastness of the hills.

II

"THE HOOT-OWL TRAIL"

Morning in the blue hills. Morning! With the slender fingers of dawn stabbing upward into a brazen sky. The chatter of a mountain jay in a pine tree. The scolding of a gray squirrel that had been disturbed at his labor of hoarding piñon nuts.

Manley gazed about him, his eyes wide with bewilderment. He was lying on a cot covered with a blanket. A tiny shaft of pale sunlight flickered in through a window of a cabin of clean logs. He breathed in the pungent odor of spruce and pine, and the pure ozone of the hills.

A man moved softly. Dale looked up into the eyes of Jim Lessert who he believed had gone to Montana after being driven from the Trionte by Wade Jeffries.

"Jim!" he exclaimed in a feeble voice.

"Yeah, that's right, Dale," the other answered softly. "Yuh shore busted into the right place, boy."

"How did I git here?"

Briefly Jim told him, and also told him of the warfare that a little company of five persecuted and dispossessed ranchers was carrying on against the man who had hounded them from their homes.

"We can't fight him in the open," Lessert explained, "so we're fightin' him under cover. We're after his payrolls and his cattle. We'll burn him out if we git a chanct. We got two more hide-outs as good as this one. If they git too hot on our trail, we'll disappear and turn up in another place."

A man entered the room, treading softly. His stern face broke into a smile when he saw that Manley was awake and conscious.

"Hyah, Dale?" he greeted.

"Howdy, Bart." Here was Jim Lessert's partner who was supposed to have given up the struggle and departed for regions unknown.

"Yuh shore had a close squeak, cowboy," Bart Connel told Manley, "but yuh'll be all right now. We had Doc Finne out from Whip Lash. Doc's a friend o' our'n and keeps our scratches patched up."

"I'm feelin' fine," remarked Manley, as he raised himself to one elbow. "Who else is here?"

"Willis Horton, Johnny Royce, and Cal Stewart. They're away now, but'll be back tonight. We got a reg'lar underground way o' gittin' information, Dale. Yuh'll be s'prised to see how many people is tyin' in with us to git Wade Jeffries. Bill Randall, the sheriff, is one of 'em."

"But this robbery and rustlin'. . . ."

Connel's dark face clouded. "We're only takin' back what's our'n, Dale. When the law goes rotten, there's only one thing honest men kin do. Might is right on the Trionte, an' we're payin' back Wade Jeffries in his own coin."

Manley learned many things during the days that he gathered strength before taking his place in the saddle. He learned that Bill Randall, the sheriff, was gathering evidence against Jeffries and was secretly aiding the dispossessed ranchers. He learned of a mysterious rider who, with black mask and black horse, took part in the raids and then disappeared.

"We don't know who he is," Lessert told Manley. "We leave a note under a rock about two miles from here, tellin' him where we're goin', and he always shows up. He only spoke once, and that was to tell us not to kill Wade Jeffries. He says that, when the time comes, Wade is his."

Johnny Royce rode in one day with information that Jeffries had put the monthly payroll in the safe at the ranch house on the Cross C.

"That money ought to be Jim's and mine," stated Connel seriously. "The ranch is still our'n even though Wade is runnin' it. I vote that we pay him a visit. Wade's payroll cash is big enough to interest 'most anybody. We shore got a right to go in our own house and open our own safe."

"Yeah, but how are we gonna blow open a safe?" Cal Stewart asked.

"That's the joke," Connel told them. "It's our ol' safe, and Johnny Royce kin open it no matter where the combination is set. He used to come over in the winter time and fool with it hours at a time, jest like a little kid with a toy gun."

Royce's huge mouth widened in a grin. "Yeah, that's

right. The ol' tin box kinda fascinated me. It gives out a faint click when it reaches the right spot. I kin open her, all right. Sometimes I think I spoiled a good safecracker to make a danged poor cowpoke."

It was long past midnight. A brilliant moon shed its white light over the prairie and turned night into day.

Six riders drew up on a hill and looked down a long, gentle slope. The silent corrals of the Cross C, with the rambling, one-story adobe house, lay spread out below them in the moonlight, a huge, misshapen scar on the dark green of the plain.

Johnny Royce spoke in a low voice. "Wade prob'ly ain't here, and I doubt if his men know the money is in the safe. He always brought it in by stage on payday so's not to put temptation in the way o' the thieves that work for him. Since we stuck up the stage and grabbed the cash, he's tryin' to sneak it in ahead o' time and thinks nobody knows it. Ernie Ross at the bank told me about it."

They trotted down the long slope, the hoof beats of the horses drumming faintly in the soft grass.

To the right of the little group rode the lone man who had joined them at the forks as they came out of the hills. Manley looked at him as he rode, without speaking, a short distance away. It seemed to him that there was something familiar about that man. He felt a vague uncertainty and uneasiness, as though an evil thing had come out of the darkness. It was a thing that could not bear the light of day, and stirred abroad only in the witching hours when graveyards yawn and give up their dead. Manley grinned at his own superstitious thought, but the feeling remained.

They drew up in the deep shadow of the house, and dismounted silently. According to a prearranged plan, Horton and Stewart remained with the horses, ready for any men who might come out through the windows. Connel would open the door with a key he had carried for years, and he would help Royce with the safe. Manley and Lessert would slip into the hall that ran between the four bedrooms where Jeffries's men would be sleeping. The masked stranger had received no orders. He did as he pleased.

The four men slipped around the house. A key grated in the lock, the sound seeming doubly loud in the silence of the night. Slowly the door swung open. They slipped into a room that was dim and ghostly in the faint light. Connel struck a match and lighted a lamp.

He and Royce went to a small, green safe standing in a corner. Royce knelt beside it and turned the combination knob.

Manley, with Lessert close behind, tiptoed to the door on the left that was standing ajar. He slipped into the hall with Lessert at his side. The discordant sound of a snore came from one of the rooms. Side-by-side the two men stood in the silent hallway.

"Put up yore hands!" A harsh command came from the room behind them. The snoring ceased. A bed creaked.

"Put 'em up high!"

Through the open door, Manley could see Royce and Connel holding up their hands. Royce was kneeling by the safe that stood open, and Connel was standing nearby.

"Wait here," Manley whispered to Lessert. He tiptoed to the doorway.

A hand and arm came into view in the lamplight. The hand was holding a blue .45.

Manley sprang into the room and faced Gar Dixon. The blue gun swerved. Manley's weapon crashed, and the blue .45 plunged to the floor, a splash of lead showing white against the cylinder.

A wild yell echoed from the hall. A gun roared, and roared again.

Manley saw Connel's weapon leap from its holster, and he sprang back into the hallway. Lessert was standing over a dark form that groaned and crawled on the floor.

"I got him, Dale!" Lessert exclaimed. "He ran out of the room and shot at me."

"Don't go out there, yuh danged fool!" cried a voice from a bedroom. "We're trapped. This way!"

The hoarse voice of Dixon shouted curses in the front room. Manley and Lessert stood waiting silently in the hallway. There came a cry and two shots from outside the house. One of the bedroom doors slammed shut, and they heard the sound of a heavy bar being dropped across it.

"It looks like one o' them *hombres* is goin' to hold the fort," Lessert threw out grimly.

Voices came from the front room, and Dale returned to it. Dixon stood close against the wall with raised hands. A man entered the room through the front door. A pair of keen eyes showed above a black mask and below a black hat drawn down over the brow. They flashed in the lamplight, and Manley shuddered with the strange feeling that had oppressed him when the man first rode out of the night.

The masked stranger stood a moment in the doorway and looked about the room. Then he withdrew silently without speaking.

Cal Stewart entered. "All's silent on the Potomac," he announced. "Three of 'em come out through the windows. Willis Horton plugged one, and the other two is backed up against the house, prayin'. What'll we do with 'em?"

"Let 'em go," answered Royce who was stuffing thick packages of green paper into a canvas bag. "We got the payroll, but we ain't got no use for Jeffries's gunnies."

Dixon was standing with eyes glued on Manley. He was cursing softly to himself. "This is the second time yuh got the best o' me, Dale Manley," he cried. "Look out for the next time, 'cause the third is the charmer."

"Yeah," Manley retorted grimly. "The third time I'll git yuh in the heart 'stead of the head. Yore head must be solid, but I want to see if yuh got a heart."

A few minutes later the angry gunnies of Wade Jeffries were left alone, the seven who had swooped down upon them riding away over the prairie that lay peacefully in the white light of the moon.

III
"DIXON LOSES HIS JOB"

It was noon of the next day. Gar Dixon, supreme among gunmen, his brow black with wrath, strode back and forth across the room, the rowels of his spurs making little clicking sounds on the floor.

Nevada Morrison and Fred Talbot watched him out of narrowing eyes. Dixon was in an ugly mood, and, when Dixon was in an ugly mood, someone was apt to die before nightfall.

"Damn Jeffries," he snarled. "Why couldn't he tell us he'd left us here to guard a safe full o' money? He don't trust us, that's what's the matter. I wisht we'd found out about it. We'd've got the money our own selves and then laid it onto this Dale Manley and his gang. Jeffries is gittin' too danged smart. He thinks he's the whole world as long as he's got us at his back. If we'd leave him, he'd be in hell in two hours. And all he pays us is a few dirty dollars a month. I'll show him. I want in on the big coin we make for him. Look what this gang done last night. Made more money in one haul than we will in a year. I'll show Jeffries he ain't so danged much! I'll fix him!"

"Yuh better not fool with Wade," interposed Talbot softly, " 'cause he's one bad *hombre,* Gar."

"Shet up!" The gunman turned fiercely upon him. "We ain't all yaller."

"But I was jest goin' to say. . . ."

"Shet up, damn yuh!" Dixon stepped toward Talbot with flaming face. "When I tell yuh I'm goin' to fix Wade Jeffries, I mean what I say. Do yuh think I'm afraid o' him? I'm tellin' yuh. . . ."

"What's the trouble, Gar?"

Wade Jeffries's cold, even voice interrupted the bellowing of the angry Dixon. The cattle king stood in the doorway. The round orifice in the barrel of his .45 was held steadily a hand's breadth above the buckle of Dixon's belt. In his other hand, Jeffries held a quirt. Several men stood back of him and crowded up to peer through the doorway.

"Put yore hands up high!" the rancher commanded.

Dixon licked his thick lips. He glanced about him hastily, and then elevated his hands.

"Unload his gun!" The order was to Talbot, who pulled Dixon's weapon from its holster, snapped out the cartridges, and returned it.

Then Jeffries stepped forward, followed closely by his men. There was a cruel smile on his thin lips.

"So yuh're goin' to fix me, are yuh?" He spoke slowly, and his words were like cold steel striking against something hard. "Yuh come to me as a gunman I could rely on in a pinch. Yuh failed me when Dale Manley beat yuh to the draw and wounded yuh in the saloon. I'm sorry he didn't kill yuh. You failed me again last night. I gather from yore remarks that yuh lost the money I put here in the safe. Now yuh want to turn against me and fix me."

The quirt shot out with a vicious smack. A red welt appeared across Dixon's face. He started forward with a bellow of rage but was brought up short by the cold voice.

"Don't move, or I'll blow yore soul to hell!"

Again and again the quirt descended. Dixon winced under the blows, but he stood motionless and kept his hands high. He was staring at the round blue hole in the barrel of Jeffries's gun.

"Now git out! Git off this range and stay off. If yuh ever come back with more of yore rotten threats, I'll strip yuh and hang yuh and leave yuh swingin' for the buzzards."

Dixon slowly dropped his hands to his sides and staggered to the door. He reached out for the jamb and stood a moment, swaying. Then he seemed to gather strength, and went out into the sunlight. A dozen grinning men watched him. He caught up his horse in the corral, saddled and bridled it with shaking hands, and then rode away without a glance backward at the man who had heaped this humiliation upon him.

For a mile or more he rode with bowed head, heedless of where the horse was taking him, careless of what the future might hold in store. The enormity of the insult sank slowly into his numbed consciousness. He, Gar Dixon, professional gunman, terror of the border for two years, possessor of a Colt .45 with six notches in the handle, had been beaten to the draw by Dale Manley, and had been horsewhipped and fired by Wade Jeffries!

He touched the burning welts across his face with shaking hand. Horsewhipped! He lifted his face to the blazing sky. The feeling of dead numbness gave way to violent, unreasoning, insane rage. He sank his spurs into the sides of his mount. He jerked viciously at the reins. Curses screamed from his drawn lips—curses that grew in foulness as they grew in volume—and he shouted crazily to the unhearing prairie and the sky.

Presently he remembered a bottle in his saddlebags. Drawing it forth, he drank a long draught of the fiery liquid. The feeling that he must return and kill Jeffries swept over him, yet he rode on and on as a sense of caution prevailed. The cattle king, surrounded by his gunmen, was safe. Dixon must wait for an opportunity. Again and again he placed the bottle to his lips.

His rage against Jeffries was no greater than his rage against Manley. These two men must die. One by one he would find them and kill them. Gar Dixon, terror of the border, had been beaten and wounded by Dale Manley. He had been horsewhipped by Wade Jeffries.

He emptied the bottle and threw it from him. He seemed to grow calmer as the whisky numbed his faculties. Swaying in the saddle, a vague plan of vengeance formed within his seething brain. Again he repeated—he must find Manley and kill him; he must catch Jeffries, alone, and kill him.

The world was turning and whirling and zigzagging about him in strange, terrifying contortions. He grasped the saddle horn to keep from falling. The horse dashed straight on over the prairie, its sides torn and bleeding from the torture it had received from the huge spurs.

Dixon knew he must stop, for everything was growing dark about him. Dimly he realized that he had drunk too much. He must sleep.

Presently a white object loomed before him that contrasted with the dark green of the prairie. Beyond it was a stream. Willows and cottonwoods lifted their heads above the plain in a winding formation as they hugged close to the living water. Dixon knew where he was. The white object was an old stone cabin that had been built and abandoned long ago by trappers or prospectors. He reached the trees and half fell from the saddle, letting the reins trail so the horse would not stray far. From habit he drew the carbine from his saddle boot, and staggered to the cabin. He wanted to lie down and sleep and forget the pain from his face, and the pain and rage within his heart.

The door sagged partly open. The gunman pushed his way into a room. There was a high, vacant window at one end. The floor was dirt, packed hard. An old cupboard was nailed against the wall of a partition, and a rough table was in the middle of the room. Dixon staggered against the table, and then went into the adjoining room. He reeled against the heavy door. It slammed shut, and a heavy bar fell across it.

The room had been a bedroom. A rough bunk stood against the wall. Dixon plunged toward it, threw himself upon it, and breathed hard through open mouth. The welts on his face burned with intense pain. He would sleep, and then go out on his trail of vengeance. Dale Manley and Wade Jeffries! Both of them must die.

He would find Jeffries first and kill him with a bullet between the eyes. He would kill Manley—with torture. The room was whirling about him. He closed his tired eyes. Presently his lips parted and his mouth opened.

Gar Dixon forgot the pain of his lashes in drunken sleep.

IV
"MANLEY FINDS A REFUGE"

Bart Connel finished counting the loot and stuffed it back into the bag.

"Right close to seven thousand simoleons," he announced. "Wade must be hirin' more'n a hundred men."

Willis Horton grinned and looked at the others. "Won't he howl when he finds out about how we got his payroll the second time?"

"Well, he ought to be satisfied if we are," drawled Connel. "He's got land and cattle enough from us to make up for it."

Manley was moving restlessly about the room. He paused and looked out of the window of the cabin. "I ain't satisfied at all," he told them. "We're jest like a bunch o' little boys with popguns, shootin' at a mountain."

"What's the matter, Dale?" Lessert asked. "Ain't our little war goin' all right?"

"No. Yuh've made a couple o' hold-ups an' got a few thousand dollars. It's chicken feed as far as Jeffries is concerned. Someday he'll surround us with his hundred men, and then he'll wipe us out like so many prairie dogs."

The others were silent for they realized there was truth in Manley's remark.

"Well, what are yuh goin' to do about it?" Lessert asked.

"I don't know, but it's got to be more'n this. I been thinkin'. Today I'm goin' to take a little scout around the Triangle Z. Jeffries stays there most o' the time. If you *hombres*'ll meet me at that old stone cabin on Cottonwood

Creek about an hour after dark, mebbe I'll have somethin' to say that'll be interestin'."

Connel spat at a box of sawdust near the table. "Dale's young and foolish and don't know when things is breakin' his way," he remarked.

"Don't yuh worry about Dale." Royce grinned as he watched the bay gelding disappear over a hill. "He knows what he's doin', and he's the fastest thing on the Trionte with a gun. We'll be at Cottonwood Creek tonight, jest as he says. Dale's got a plan."

As a matter of fact, Manley's plan was vague. First he intended to locate a large herd of Jeffries's cattle. Many of them belonged to the ranchers, but Jeffries, in his lawless way, simply vented the brands and put on his own iron.

Manley thought vaguely of making a great raid upon the cattle, of driving them at night through Sangre Pass, and of turning them over to Shark Higgins on the other side of the divide. Shark had handled the herd of three-year-olds the men already had driven through the pass.

The cowboy had a twelve-mile ride ahead to the Triangle Z. There would be plenty of time to rest the horse an hour, or even more, before going to the rendezvous at the stone cabin.

A cold rage filled his heart as he rode past the charred ruins of his own little spread. A dozen yearlings that he recognized as his were gathered around a spring that bubbled, clear and cold, out of the side of a hill. There was a vent across the Flying Q brand, and on the shoulders flamed the new red scar of the Triangle Z.

Jeffries not only took the cattle of the ranchers as he drove them from their land, but he appropriated them without even attempting to cover up the theft.

The only official in the county he did not own was square-shooting Bill Randall, the sheriff, and Randall was helpless against the power of the monarch of the Trionte. What could a lone sheriff do against a man with a hundred gun rannies at his back? It was not without reason that Jeffries considered himself above the law.

The sudden vicious snarl of a bullet suddenly jerked Manley from his reverie.

A drumming of hoofs sounded on the trail to the right, and a dozen or more men dashed toward him in a close body. With a hasty glance he recognized Jeffries, Walters, and Travis, the deputy sheriff who backed Jeffries in his lawless rule of the range.

A moment later the bay gelding was skimming the prairie. He was headed straight for the hills that were blue and hazy in the distance. Bullets from high-powered rifles snarled past, until a burst of speed on the part of the gelding put them out of range.

Manley settled down to the long race for the hills, for the men behind showed no signs of abandoning the chase. He did not fear the result. He knew the gelding could outdistance the mounts that were hot on the trail.

Steadily he drew ahead of his pursuers. Slowly the bay gelding widened the gap between them.

A white speck on the landscape grew larger and then metamorphosed into the old stone cabin. Past it wound the green line of trees that grew along the edge of Cottonwood Creek. Beyond it rose the blue hills that bounded on the west the kingdom where the will of Wade Jeffries was law.

The gelding stumbled and went to its knees. Manley was almost pitched over its head. Bravely the splendid animal staggered to its feet and went on. It limped badly, and Manley knew it had stepped into a grass-covered badger hole. Often a horse's leg was broken with such a fall.

A triumphant shout rang out across the prairie. Manley looked backward with wildly beating heart. Jeffries and his men had gained. Manley knew he could not reach the hills. Even now the cruelty of riding an injured horse cut him to the heart. Straight to the stone cabin he raced, the courageous bay holding the pace without flinching. A bullet *whined* past, and then another. The men were dashing forward desperately in an attempt to cut him off from the shelter of the cabin.

Manley could see the front door sagging on its hinges. If he could reach it, he would have a chance. He could be attacked only from one side of the cabin—from Cottonwood Creek with its thick brush and trees.

"Come on, boy!" he shouted, and the bay plunged forward in a last desperate spurt.

Closer and closer they came to the cabin. Bullets *whizzed* about them like angry hornets as the pursuers fired in the hope of scoring a hit before Manley could reach shelter.

A moment later he rode up before the door, yanked the rifle from the saddle boot, and plunged through the doorway. He fired twice at Jeffries who turned and headed straight for the trees.

Manley jammed the sagging door shut and blocked it by moving the old table against it. The high, narrow window faced the creek. He felt there was a chance to stand off the men until dark. If only they did not charge him in a body, or reach him with a bullet!

He knew the cabin would soon be the target for as hot a fire as twelve or fifteen expert riflemen could lay down, that bullets would smash through window and walls, seeking out every hole that relentless time had made in the mud chinks between the rough stones.

V
"BESIEGED"

Dale Manley looked about him. He realized there was not much shelter behind those stone walls with the wide chinks stopped with soft clay. The table was the only furniture except a rude cupboard, backless and rotted, that was nailed against the partition that divided the cabin.

What was in the other room? Dale needed some heavy furniture that could be stood against the wall, something that would give additional shelter from the hot lead that would rake the cabin from end to end.

He started to the door between the rooms. A bullet whipped in through the window. Its *whine* was echoed by the muffled report of a rifle from the trees. The cowboy dashed back to the wall. Peering cautiously out at the edge of the window, he pushed the muzzle of his rifle over the weather-beaten sill.

There was a slight movement in the brush at the edge of the stream.

Crash!

A man cried out hoarsely. He sprang to his feet, clawed the air, and pitched forward.

A dead silence followed. Then the prairie echoed to the driving, crashing drum of relentless, steady gunfire.

A thin tongue of flame shot out from a dense growth of willows, and Manley fired, aiming a little behind the flash. A man ducked back into the trees, and the cowboy swore softly to himself. He moved away from the window and knelt close to the wall in a corner. A hail of bullets smashed through the window, chipping splinters from the ancient casing. The clay chinking in the walls fell inward in lumps that gave off a dust as fine as smoke. A jagged hole appeared between the stones near Manley's head. After a moment, he peered through it. Streaks of orange flame pierced out from the shadows of the trees, sharp, quick streaks that flamed death at the little cabin.

Manley whipped up his rifle and fired through the hole. Then he lay flat and wriggled to the other corner. He knew he must keep moving in this unequal struggle. Every shot would bring back a fusillade of lead from those who were seeking his blood.

Steadily, relentlessly, the bullets tore into the cabin. Manley lay flat behind two large stones that had only a fine seam between them. He was comparatively safe there if his enemies did not charge the cabin. He did not know exactly how many were out there in the shelter of the trees. A dozen at least, not counting the man he had killed or wounded. He counted five spurts of flame at different places to the left. Four more came from directly ahead. He could not tell how many there were at the right, but it looked as though there were seven or eight.

The rifles crashed steadily from the woods. The window casing was a wreck now, and gaping holes appeared in the wall. One of them was low, down near the floor. Manley rolled to it. Straight ahead from a clump of bushes came the sharp *crack* of a gun. Thin wisps of smoke curled up in the still, dead air.

Into those bushes Manley poured his fire. His lips were set, and he swore softly as he yanked at the lever of his Winchester. He kept no count of his shots till the *click* of hammer against firing pin told him that the magazine was empty. With quick fingers he fed bullets through the slide.

He didn't know if he had winged his man, but he intended to show them he was still alive and kicking.

The thought gave him an idea. Springing to his feet, he fired twice through the window, and then fell flat. A hail of bullets poured into the cabin above him. Then he cried out with a long, wailing cry.

The firing ceased. Manley could hear indistinct voices in the woods. They were exultant voices that called to one another with coarse jest.

Carefully the cowboy pushed the muzzle of his gun through a gaping hole in the wall. He waited silently. The minutes dragged by. There was no movement or sound from among the trees.

Finally a gray hat appeared above a thick buffalo bush. The cowboy grinned. He was not quite simple enough to be deceived by that trick. A head came into view, but Manley still held his fire. Another and another poked out between the thick branches. None of them belonged to Jeffries, the man he was seeking.

A man started forward, running toward the cabin. Evidently he was ambitious to finish the killing, if any finish were needed.

Manley brought his rifle to his shoulder, drew a fine sight on the moving right leg, and squeezed the trigger. The bullet stopped the man as he came head on. He flung face down, rolled over twice, and lay without moving. Manley knew he was not dead. He snapped two more shots at the men showing in the trees, but they dodged back, and he did not know if his fire had been effective.

For an hour or more Jeffries's gunnies poured shot after shot into the stone house. A red, distorted sun sank toward the horizon and touched the peaks of the blue hills. The round, red orb of the moon was visible in the eastern sky.

If Manley could hold out two hours longer, his friends would come. He wished they knew now that he was there waiting for them. If they should ride up on the other side of the stream, they would catch Jeffries and his men between two fires. And yet, after all, the range king who had outlawed the law might be too strong for them. They would be outnumbered two to one.

As though by order, the firing ceased. Manley lay at his porthole and looked out into the rapidly deepening twilight. He knew his enemies were up to something. Those men would not give up a fight against one man as long as the cattle king, thirsting for vengeance, was there to drive them on.

Presently he saw three men walk out of the trees far to the left, and as many more to the right. They were beyond gun range. Manley knew they were surrounding the cabin and would creep up as darkness fell. In the dim light it was no longer necessary for them to remain under cover of the trees.

Desperately the cowboy looked about him. He must cover all sides of the cabin at once. He rose to his feet and stepped softly to the door between the rooms. It was locked.

A bullet whipped in through the window and *spanged* against the wall within a foot of his head. Cursing softly, he sank to the floor and crawled back to his place. If Jeffries and his men came from the other side, Manley must meet them kneeling in a corner of the room. He would try and give a good account of himself before he died.

His lips twisted in a pathetic grin. What a surprise would await the boys if they came to the cabin in time. Here was their chance of meeting the man who had driven them like dogs from their ranches. Instead, perhaps, they would find only a shattered cabin, and Dale Manley's still body lying in the soft moonlight.

Prone on the floor, the cowboy shot with a slow deliberation at every flash that stabbed out from the trees. The sharp *spang* of his rifle echoed back from the green wall at the edge of the stream.

He listened for the sound of firearms from the other side of the cabin. Presently it came—a quick, muffled drumming of steady firing. From the adjoining room sounded the low snarl of a human voice that rose in volume and ended in a hoarse curse.

Manley sprang to his feet in surprise. There was someone in the other room of the cabin!

VI

"A STRANGE ALLY"

The snarling growl continued. Then Manley was startled by a *boom*—the unmistakable discharge of a carbine. Again and again the gun roared. Whoever the man in the next room might be, he had come to Manley's aid at an opportune time.

The cowboy knelt close to the wall. Hope had taken the place of the dull despair that had obsessed him during the long struggle. It was not only the aid from the unknown in the next room. Manley's courage revived from the fact that a friend was behind him, and that he was not alone in his battle against the gunmen of Wade Jeffries.

He placed a steady stream of bullets into the trees, aiming just behind the orange flashes flaming in the twilight that deepened as the struggle raged. He wondered how he could have escaped unscathed from the bullets that had smashed their way into the cabin through the long afternoon.

Slowly a wide patch of silver moonlight formed on the wall behind him. Then he saw them—five riders close together coming over a slight rise. Another was a short distance away. His friends had come! The mysterious masked rider was with them. He watched them all pull up and stop. Evidently they were surprised at the ring of rifle fire, and the two guns that barked vicious answers from the cabin. If only Manley could tell them the situation. If only they knew that their enemy was before them! Then it occurred to him that he could use the distress signal that Jim Lessert had shown him. If any member of their little body was in danger, he could fire three times quickly, and then once more after a short pause. Manley threw up his rifle.

Crack, crack, crack! Interval. *Crack!*

Twice he repeated the signal. He knew the stabs of flame would be visible to his friends even though the reports might be merged with the steady fire around him. He loaded the rifle again and suddenly realized that his ammunition was running low.

He could see the ranchers spread out into a half-circle and ride downward to the stream two or three hundred yards below the cabin.

Evidently they had not been seen by Jeffries and his men, for the bullets still poured steadily into the cabin from all sides. The carbine in the next room roared out its challenge. Occasionally a hoarse voice jeered out a dare to Jeffries to come on. Whoever the man was, he was no coward. It seemed to Manley, too, that somewhere he had heard that voice.

Again the cowboy poured his shots into the trees,

moving from place to place as the answering fire tore through the cracks in the wall and *spanged* against the stones. He pulled the last shell from his belt and shoved it through the slide. Four shots were left for the rifle, and there were six in his .44. Both rifle and revolver took the same ammunition.

He fired twice, and then watched the drama that was being acted out on the prairie. His friends reached the timber some distance below the scene of the fight. Doubtless, they would creep up under cover and catch Jeffries's men in a quick, furious charge. The gunnies out on the prairie had no horses, and could be attended to later.

Manley wanted to shout in his exultation. A grim fate seemed to be working for him.

He drew his six-gun and pulled the trigger. Its deep roar contrasted with the sharp *crack* of the long-barreled rifle. Again and again the roar shattered the stillness. Short of ammunition though he might be, he wanted to hold the attention of the men in the trees.

A sudden cheer sounded from the stream. A *crash* of gunfire followed. Seven men dashed out into the open in a straggling line, and came straight toward the cabin. Wade Jeffries's men had been flushed from cover, but Manley found himself in his greatest danger of the day. These men must not gain the cabin and take possession.

His gun jerked twice. The second bullet stopped one of the men as he dashed forward. He fell headlong and rolled over. Manley recognized Travis, who was the crooked deputy sheriff.

The others came on. Again Manley fired, and then dropped his .44 as the last shot was spent.

Crack!

Another man went down as Manley threw up his rifle

and fired the two shots remaining. He saw the five men turn and dash around the cabin some distance away.

Breathing a sigh of relief, he realized he was safe for the moment. He was conscious of the firing outside. He looked through the window and saw the sharp stabs of flame leaping out from the trees. This time they were not aimed at the cabin, but at the men afoot who were dodging about on the prairie. The attackers had become the attacked. His friends had captured the horses and held the situation in hand.

A door creaked, and Manley turned. In the doorway, his burly form and flushed face plain in the moonlight that flooded the room, stood Gar Dixon. Manley stared at the .45 that the gunman held in his hand.

For long moments the two men stood looking at each other. The livid welts across Dixon's face showed black in the light of the moon.

"Dale Manley, by hell!" the gunman leered. "I got yuh at last. Yuh beat me to the draw! Me, Gar Dixon! Yuh shot the gun out o' my hand last night. The man don't live that does that. Say yore prayers, cowboy, 'cause I'm shootin' at the count o' ten. Go for yore gun an' see what happens." He began counting in a low voice.

Manley looked into the beastly face before him. Unarmed, he had no chance against the enraged gunman who had been the terror of the border.

"Four . . . five . . . six. . . ." Dixon counted slowly as though he were chanting a death song.

From outside the cabin came the steady crashing of rifles in the hands of desperate men.

"Seven . . . eight . . . nine. . . ."

Manley sprang. Dixon's weapon was pointed a few inches above the cowboy's belt buckle.

The hammer fell, but there was no report. Dixon had forgotten, in his rage and drunken stupor, that his six-gun had been emptied by Talbot at the command of Wade Jeffries.

Like a raging demon, Manley came on. His fist smashed into the red face before him. Dixon staggered back through the doorway. Recovering, he stooped quickly, and a knife flashed out of his boot top. He lunged forward.

Manley dodged and avoided the sweep of the keen blade by a hair. His fist shot out and smacked against the side of the gunman's head. With a bellow of rage, Dixon turned. Again the blade flashed in the moonlight. A searing pain shot along the cowboy's side. He seized Dixon's wrist in his left hand and smashed into the leering face with his right.

Dixon howled with pain and rage. Blood spouted from his nose. Again and again Manley smashed into the face before him. He clung desperately to Dixon's wrist, trying to twist it and make the gunny drop the knife. Dixon smashed out with his fist, and a flash of flame seemed to envelop the room as Manley was taken fairly between the eyes.

Grimly, furiously, they clinched and stood, straining every muscle. Knee to knee, their teeth clenched, their muscles stood out like ropes with their Gargantuan efforts. Manley was fighting for his life, and he knew he was fighting against a more powerful man than himself. Only his lithe quickness saved him again and again. Dixon wrenched his knife hand free. He raised the blade high for the blow that would finish the struggle. Again Manley caught the wrist, and Dixon bellowed a curse.

Manley threw his right arm around the huge waist and tried to trip the gunman. A big fist came down again and again on his face and unprotected head. The blows hurt, but Dale Manley gritted his teeth and wrenched and tore at the barrel of a body that was hard as nails. Like a leech, he clung to the waist that held the flashing blade.

They crashed into the table that was propped against the door, and nearly went down. Desperately Manley tried to throw his antagonist, and desperately Dixon struggled to free his knife hand.

The shooting on the outside of the cabin stopped suddenly, but the two did not notice the strange silence that followed the long afternoon and evening of constant gunfire.

Dixon lunged forward with a herculean effort that bent Manley backward over the table. Curses spewed from the gunman's lips. Desperately he struck downward at Manley's head.

The cowboy threw out a leg and felt it touch Dixon's behind the knee. He threw all his strength into a desperate heave. Dixon was thrown off balance and went down flat on his back. A terrible cry rent the silence of the night. Dixon rose upward with a frenzied movement, then sank back and lay still. Manley knew the gunman had fallen on the knife.

He stood panting with his terrible exertions. His shirt was torn from his back. Blood was streaming down his face, and his clothing was wet from the wound in his side. He heard voices from outside the cabin. He pushed the table to one side, jerked open the door, and then staggered weakly out into the moonlight.

VII
"THE MASKED STRANGER"

Wade Jeffries stood there defiantly. His head was bare, and he was unarmed. Jim Lessert and Cal Stewart were at his side.

Far off across the plain, four or five men were hastening away on foot. They were the last of the gunnies who had chased Manley to this place. The ground was dotted at intervals with the still forms of the others.

Far to the right something seemed to be moving against the horizon, but Manley gave it not a thought as he watched the drama that was unfolding before him. Wade Jeffries was speaking. Cool, collected, his thin, handsome face seemed doubly pale in the white light.

"All right, yuh got me," he was saying, "and I'll give in. Yuh can't kill me in cold blood, so I'm willin' to do my share. I'll give yuh back yore ranches and stock, and pay for the damage. How's that?"

"How do we know yuh won't run us out again as soon as we turn yuh loose?" asked Connel.

"I'll fire my gunnies and hire honest cowboys. I'll put up a peace bond of a hundred thousand dollars, and the war will be over for good."

Perhaps Jeffries was more frightened than he appeared to be, for his proposition was better than anyone there would have expected.

"If yuh don't trust me," he went on, "I'll buy yuh out at a fair price. We'll have ever'thing appraised by cattlemen from the other side of the divide, and I'll pay whatever

they say. Ain't that fair?"

Bart Connel turned to the others. "Yuh all heard it," he stated. "Has anybody any objections?"

"I have!"

The voice rang out like a pistol shot in the still night. The masked stranger stepped forward into the circle.

Manley shuddered as he looked again at that cloaked form. Again he had the feeling that here was a being sprung from the grave, and that he had no fit place in a world of sunlight and shadow and beauty.

The man's hand went to his head, and the mask fell. He turned his face full to the brilliant moon.

The sight of that face sent a shiver of horror crinkling up and down Manley's spine. Once seen, it was a face that never could be forgotten—a face that would haunt a man's dreams to his dying day.

Evidently, at some time, the man had fallen face downward into a fire. He had been burned and blackened and scarred beyond the resemblance to a human being. The tiny, peaked, misshapen nose looked as though it had been formed by some amateur surgeon. The lips were twisted into a mirthless smile. It disclosed teeth that flashed in the light of the moon. It was a perpetual and ghastly smile. Strange to behold, the eyes were undamaged, and they were large and bright in the setting of that frightful face.

No one spoke or moved.

"Yuh don't know me," the man said after a pause, "but I'm yore old neighbor, Dan Morgan. I am one of the victims of that man."

He pointed a finger at Wade Jeffries who started back and drew in his breath with a hissing sound.

"I had a wife," the man continued. "She was young and beautiful and didn't understand. This man ruined her life

as well as mine. She is now in Juárez, drug-crazed and dyin'. He tried to kill me, and left me for dead in the fire. I was rescued by an old prospector who had been a surgeon. He saved my life for this night. Wade Jeffries, I have come for yuh."

"What do yuh want?" The cattle king's voice was scarcely above a whisper.

"I want you. Give him his gun, men. I ask it, and I have the right to ask. We will stand together, back to back, and at the count we will go ten paces forward. Then we will turn and fire. I'm givin' him a fair chance for his long-ago forfeited life."

Manley stood weakly against the cabin. As in a dream he saw the two men standing back to back, each with a drawn gun in his hand.

Bart Connel counted. "One . . . two . . . three . . . ," he began.

It was the second time that night that Manley had heard that slow count.

Both men started forward.

"Four . . . five . . . six. . . ."

Again Manley noticed the dark mass moving over the prairie. He wondered if more of Wade's men were coming. He wanted to cry out, but his tongue seemed glued to the roof of his mouth.

"Seven . . . eight. . . ."

Jeffries whirled. A stab of red flame shot out from his gun, and the *crash* rang out on the still night.

Morgan stumbled and fell. Jeffries jumped backward a pace and held the others at the point of his waving gun.

"Don't move!" he cried. "I'll shoot the first one that. . . ."

Spang!

It was the crack of a gun in the hand of the prone Morgan. Jeffries spun halfway around. Again his gun flamed, but this time the bullet went into the ground before him as his knees buckled and he fell at full length.

Manley staggered to Morgan's side. The man's eyes were very bright in the moonlight.

"Is . . . is Jeffries dead?" he gasped.

"He shore is," came the voice of Johnny Royce. "Shot plumb through the heart."

"Dale," Morgan gasped, "you were our friend. Find her . . . in Juárez. Tell her . . . tell her . . . I killed him . . . man to man. Tell . . . her . . . I'll be . . . waitin'. . . ."

The sentence ended in a rattle. Dan Morgan had died the death of a man.

The roll of many hoofs sounded on the prairie, and a group of fifty or more men rode up. At the head was Randall, the square-shooting sheriff.

"What's this, men?" he asked as he looked about him.

Briefly Bart Connel explained.

"I brought this posse from the other side o' the divide," the sheriff told them. "I got the evidence clear against Jeffries, and was after him to bring him to trial."

He looked about him, and then removed his hat.

"Yore war is over with Wade Jeffries," he announced in a low voice, "and peace has come back to the Trionte. I guess it's best that way."

Mules

Do a man a favor—thought Sanders—*and he's as likely as not to expect you to take care of him the rest of his life.* Just as now, for instance, Sanders's Mojave law office seemed once more in danger of becoming headquarters for the lank, unregenerate figure known from one end of the desert to the other as Twenty-Mule Bill.

"What's the matter now?" Sanders demanded.

There was injury in Bill's blue eyes, and accusation in the droop of his mustache when he spoke. "Mister Sanders," he said, "I'm looking for work. And I would appreciate to get hold of the loan of five dollars."

"Looking for work?" Sanders repeated. "What's the matter with the job I got you three weeks ago, freighting for the Smoky Glory?"

Bill sighed. "Mister Sanders, I am pained to state it was the same old story. I got run out."

"I'm going to give you up," Sanders said. "Here you are, the best jerk-line driver in three states . . . about the only one left that can handle a twenty-mule hitch with distinction . . . and here I get you one more job, and you even blow that! What was the complaint this time?"

"Mister Sanders, they claim I choked off the town of Coyote Wells. I can't go back there any more."

"You mean you got boiled and shot up the town?"

"Oh, no . . . nothing superficial like that. Coyote Wells is choked off right at the root this time. You know, that town ain't got any excuse except the Smoky Glory mine is behind it . . . no mine, no town. And the mine has about gone out of business since I left."

"But, Bill, how the dickens could you, single-handed, put a ten million dollar property out of business?"

"Why, that, Mister Sanders, was due to the Smoky Glory losing them mules. Ab Mackenzie . . . it seems like he has an affinity for mules or something. Maybe that's how come he's boss of the Smoky Glory. Anyway, he won't give an inch when it comes to a question of mules. So now the railroad won't haul no high-grade until Mackenzie settles up . . . and Mackenzie won't settle up until the railroad hauls the high-grade. The Smoky Glory can't pay off until the ore is hauled, and business has become very stagnant and depressed around there . . . I never seen such an exasperated lot of people. It sure looks like the mining business is a thing of the past at Coyote Wells. And the railroad aims to sue the Smoky Glory about the mules."

"But . . . look here! What have lost mules to do with the railroad suing the Smoky Glory?"

"I'll tell you about it," Bill said courteously, "if only you'll be so kind, sir, please, sir, as to shut your damn' yap, enough to listen like a reasonable man. After I'd been working for the Smoky Glory about two days"—Twenty-Mule Bill went on—"Ab Mackenzie begun to depend on me a lot. Naturally the best twenty-mule jerk-line driver in the country, me, is an awful valuable man around a dump like that. So I was naturally the one Mackenzie picked out to go down to New Ballarat to straighten out the mule mystery.

"It seems that Mackenzie had been expecting a team of mules in by freight, and he had just found out that his mule team had got only as far as the siding at New Ballarat.

Seems like at New Ballarat all them leatherheads had took wings or something, for that was the last anybody had heard tell of them mules. My job was to go down and solve the mystery . . . the mystery principally being who the heck had fastened onto our long team.

"Well, Mister Sanders, I went to New Ballarat by fast freight, and I sized up the situation. It seems Mackenzie had sent Tonopah Shorty down to bring this team upcountry in a cow car. Shorty had loaded his mules down in the Imperial all right, and managed to get hooked onto a freight. And they started upcountry all regular and serene, the mules riding inside the cow car and Shorty riding on top, to feed hay and water such as mules almost continually require. So far, so good.

"But at New Ballarat it seems that Shorty let the situation get out of hand. His cow car of mules bust loose from the freight, and run up a siding, and made a thing of the past out of a bunk car belonging to a railroad grading outfit that was working there. And that would have been all right, too, and served the railroad right. Only, about half the slats got ripped off of the cow crate, and those darn' mules sallied out and lit for open country.

"I looked up Shorty. He had got hold of some forty rod, and he was punishing it severely. I asked him why he hadn't rounded up his mules, and he said it was because he was discouraged. When they hit the bunk car, Shorty flew off the top and lit in some Fresno scrapers, and it discouraged him. I got that much out of Shorty before he went back to sleep on me. I woke him up again and tried to show him it was his duty to come and help round up the stock, but he said he'd resigned and guessed he would retire on the county. And that was all I got out of him.

"Well, I looked around New Ballarat, and I hired a

fellow name of Slim Hinkle to help out, and me and Slim set out to round up them wandering harness canaries.

"I suppose you realize, Mister Sanders, that a twenty-mule team is made up of eighteen mules and two horses. Me and Slim found the two horses right off. But when it come to those eighteen mules. . . .

"Mister Sanders, I went through hell making the gather of them mules. We couldn't find 'em.

" 'Slim,' I says, 'Ab Mackenzie is an impetuous man. If we don't get him back his leatherheads, he is sure liable to view this thing in an unfavorable light. We got to round up that stock if it takes us hours.'

"Hours, hell! It took us close onto a week!

"In some ways them was the most stirring days of my life. What you don't realize, Mister Sanders, is that a man gets somewhat saddle-sore, after he hasn't rode for a couple years. It's only the last couple of days, Mister Sanders, that I have so recovered that I can sit down comfortable.

"And to make things worse, the grading outfit moved fifteen miles down the track after the first day, depriving us of the sole place for bumming meals. If ever men made a supreme effort in behalf of their brand, it was me and Slim after them mules. I want you to understand that distinctly, Mister Sanders.

"Because in the end we foozled. I have to own up to the truth. It ain't happened often, Mister Sanders . . . there's very few times in my life that I've had to admit that I fell down. But finally, when we got word we would have to hook our cow cage onto the next freight, the mule chorus was still shy one tenor voice, valued at forty dollars.

" 'Slim,' says I, 'this lost jughead has busted my spirit. This is a good job, Slim . . . but you take it. Go ahead and ride to Coyote Wells on the cow Pullman and explain to Ab

Mackenzie that the seventeen mules we rounded back was probably the pick o' the lot.'

" 'Not much,' says Slim. 'I'll help you load stock, but after that . . . eight dollars, please! I'm done.'

"And furthermore, our troubles had only begun. What you don't realize, Mister Sanders, is that it's no child's play to load mules, especially in them little short cars they give you nowadays. You take a mule in a sitting position at the bottom of a steep plank by hand, and you try to shoot him up that plank by hand, and, I tell you, you'll find it very tiring, Mister Sanders, in the course of a forenoon. I had kind of counted on talking the gang from the grading outfit into elevating them brutes up into the car, but, wouldn't you know it, they was a long ways off by this time, like I said.

"The worst of it was, those were awful big swivel-ears, Mister Sanders. I never seen such whoppers. Toward the end it got to be a bad problem to fit them things in there.

"But we loaded 'em, Mister Sanders. I'm proud to say we done it. I even kind of persuaded myself that Ab Mackenzie would maybe overlook the lack of that one other mule, seeing all the work I'd been put to about the rest.

"Mister Sanders, that hope was one of these holler shells. That train run the two hundred and fifty miles to Coyote Wells awful slow, but not by no means slow enough to suit me. The hour and the day finally come when I had to stand before Ab Mackenzie and state that I was one heavy-gauge jack rabbit shy.

" 'Mister Mackenzie,' said I, 'frankly, I have went to work and fell down on you. Seventeen mules was every last mule I could dig up.'

"Mister Sanders, what use is it to try to get sympathy and understanding from a wild-eyed Scotchman that is nuts about mules? I answer you that it ain't any use.

"So there's the story, Mister Sanders. You now know the whole thing of how come the Smoky Glory has fired its best twenty-mule jerk-line man, me, and the railroad is suing Ab Mackenzie, and Ab Mackenzie has got one of his stubborn streaks, and the whole end of the desert is tied up in a hard knot."

"Twenty-mule Bill," said Sanders after a short period devoted to thought, "I must say your story is unclear in the extreme. I can see how Mackenzie might have a case against the railroad, but exactly how can the railroad sue Mackenzie?"

"Why, it seems," Bill explained, "that this construction outfit, being out of commission at just the wrong time, tied up the line, and there was forty carloads of melons that couldn't get through. And those melons, being tied up in the desert so long, they claim cost the railroad. . . ."

"But how in time," Sanders demanded, "could the railroad construction outfit be put out of commission by the fact that Mackenzie lost a mule?"

"What mule?"

"You said you got out of New Ballarat with seventeen mules."

"Oh, yeah, that's right. But damn the luck! That was just the trouble. That construction gang can holler all they want, Mister Sanders, but no man can say I ain't top champion when it comes to rounding up lost stock. You see, we was two hundred and fifty miles down the track, and them seventeen compressed mules was unloaded and the car sent on, before we found out that Shorty had only had six mules in that cow crate to start out with."

"Six to start with, and seventeen to end up . . . look here . . . you mean you . . . ?"

"Mister Sanders, am I supposed to be able to come up with a mule in the desert and tell who he belongs to just by reading his mind? And is it my fault if the construction outfit was the only other people around there using mules? It wasn't until this construction argument came up that I found out why I could never get hold of that last mule I thought I needed."

"Why?"

"Come to find out, I'd already accidentally picked up all the mules that construction gang had."

The Killer in the Chute

In some ways that rodeo at Las Cruces was one of the funniest I ever saw. It seemed like everybody was always ready to fight at the drop of a hat, so that it was very seldom that an hour went by without a brawl going on some place. There is always some scrapping behind the scenes at a rodeo, but during this show we had fighting all the time, until you would have doubted if cowboys were really peaceable men after all.

The funny thing was that nobody seemed to know just what he was sore about, or if he thought he knew, it was no good reason, and no two reasons alike. But as I think back now, I believe it was because of the way the Helmholtz brothers horned in that year and sort of took over that rodeo, until there was a kind of shadow of them all over the whole darned works.

These four Helmholtz brothers had started out in cattle, and got kind of halfway into banking, and ended up with a cattle loan company business that was now likely to own more cattle than any three outfits in the state. Now, I've seen plenty of cattle taken up to meet loans, and the people who lost their cattle were often some displeased, and I don't know exactly what was different about the way the Helmholtz brothers did business.

But I don't think you can find anybody who will admit he ever got a square deal from those Helmholtzes, and I suppose half the cattlemen in the state had a knife honing for that outfit. So you can see why it made everybody feel rollicky to have these Helmholtz brothers come in and start out to run the Las Cruces rodeo, and get away with it, too, for a little while.

I was sitting on a bale of hay, back of the chutes, the day before the rodeo began, talking to Whiskers Beck and Ben Cord. And they were giving me a few reasons why they had gone sour on the Helmholtz outfit. It seems that Ben and Whiskers Beck were the only two riders left to Johnny Fraser and his Star Loop outfit up on the Tonto Rim. Johnny was a good kid and a white man, but the Helmholtzes had got him tied where he stood to lose the whole works—what of it the Helmholtzes hadn't grabbed already. I wish now I had listened closer, for, if I had, maybe I would be able to explain to you better what happened.

But just then I was thinking about something else. You see, I knew Ben Cord pretty well, or did once, but I had never seen Whiskers Beck before. And I had a special reason for wanting to get to know him.

Whiskers Beck was a bald old cowboy, with white whiskers that were short but very bushy. While I knew him, he always wore a wool brush jacket with big black and white checks, and held up his Levi's pants with a four-inch leather belt with big silver conchos on it. But what interested me was that I understood this old boy had a running horse cached in the bushes, and was figuring to run him in the 440 that was coming off the second day of the rodeo.

I had brought a little sprint horse to this rodeo myself. So Whiskers Beck and I were sizing each other up, each one of us trying to figure out what he was up against in the case of the other fellow's horse. The upshot of it was that by and by Whiskers and I agreed there wasn't any use of cow folks like us fighting among each other, so we just took our ponies off in the brush and tried them out.

As it worked out, both of us were kind of disappointed in the little difference between our two horses, and I may as well say right now that neither one of us ever ran his horse in that quarter-mile race. But that was how it came about that I got to be a very close friend—and you might say a partner for a little while—of Whiskers Beck.

"You and me might as well figure to split second money, if any at all," I told him. "There's a feller here has a pony that can beat us both from here to Tuesday."

Whiskers was terrible let-down because his pony had not stood out against mine the way he'd hoped and figured.

"Darned if I know where I'm going to head in," he said, very hopeless. "Some way or another I've got to make an awful lot of money out of this rodeo show."

"How much money do you call a lot?"

He looked me over very cool. "About five thousand *pesos*," he said at last.

I looked at him with pity.

"Maybe," said Whiskers Beck, "I can rouse up a few good odds against Ben Cord taking first money in the bronc' riding."

I started to tell him he was crazy, but I let it pass. This Ben Cord was a good husky kid, maybe thirteen years old. He was half Indian, but one of the best built men I ever saw—long in the legs and thin in the middle, with a chest like a barrel and shoulders fit for an ox. He had a head like a lion, wide-set eyes, high cheek bones, and all cut very square out of one piece. But when it came to riding, I knew Ben was just a fair to average bucking horse rider. As we went back to the corrals I was feeling sorry for Whiskers Beck, and figuring on how much I could do for myself by taking up some of those bets that Whiskers was so anxious to lay.

Then as we were walking past the bucking horse corral, a thing happened that was going to change the whole dope on that rodeo, and Whiskers Beck's plans, and mine, too, though I didn't fully understand all about that right away.

Just as we were passing the corral, a horse let out a bawl, and there was some hoof hammering and a cracking sound like a horse kicking a six-inch post right out of the ground. You are always hearing that kind of row around the bronc's, but this time there was a minute of silence right after that, as if everything within earshot suddenly stood to listen. Out of that sudden quiet we heard somebody yell: "In God's name, kill him! Hasn't anybody got a gun?"

Then noise began—horses milling, people running and shouting, and the *snap* of a rope end.

We ran over to where a little part of the bronc' corral was divided off, and they were keeping a big black horse in the small part alone. Somebody had dabbed a loop over the fence and got this black horse around the neck, and he and three or four cowboys took on to the end of the rope and was choking him. The heavy barred fence shook like it was going to come down as they tried to hold that horse.

The big black went straight up in the air, pawing at the rope, then came down on his back. Then I saw that a couple of other boys had jumped into the corral and were dragging something out under the lower bar of the fence.

Pretty soon I found out that this they dragged out had been a good little rider named Bob Dennis, but he would never scratch bronc's any more.

Whiskers Beck and Ben and I went over and stood looking at that big black horse kind of gloomy, the way a man looks at a horse that has just killed a man.

"Boy, boy," said Ben Cord, "I'd give anything I got to draw that pony in the contest!"

Whiskers said, very dull and flat: "What horse is that?"

"That's Pain Killer," I told him. "I know that horse. He bucked me down in three jumps at Cheyenne. Pain whirled and jumped to come down on me, but Bill Daly jumped his horse across me and rammed him. Pain reared up and struck Bill out of the saddle and broke his arm."

"Funny name for a horse," said Whiskers Beck.

"It's a joke," I explained to him. "The first man he killed was named Payne."

"You think that's a funny joke?" said Whiskers Beck.

I was feeling kind of sick, but I had always thought it was funny up to now, so I stuck to it. "Sure, that's funny," I said.

Whiskers Beck started to say—"Well, I. . . ." Then all of a sudden he grabbed hold of one of the bars of the fence, and stared inside at the big black as if he would jump through the fence and bite him.

I saw the knuckles of his hands turn white on the fence bar.

"Whiskers, what's the matter with you?"

"Gil," said Whiskers, "my eyes ain't so good as they was. Look at that horse for me. Look on the inside of his off gaskin . . . and tell me what you see."

"I see a half moon scar, like from a wire cut," I told him.

Whisker Beck's voice was awful quick, but still it kind of quavered. "Gil," he said, "I know that horse! That's a Stillwater country horse."

"He belongs to the Helmholtz brothers now," I said.

"So I heard," Whiskers Beck mumbled so I could hardly hear him. "Yeah, I heard that. Only I didn't realize. . . ." Whiskers Beck drummed on the bar of the fence for a minute with the side of his fist. Then all of a sudden he turned, and he walked away.

"He's got a hate on those Helmholtz brothers," Ben said, "on account of Johnny."

Still I didn't see why old Whiskers should take it so hard just to find out that the Helmholtzes had a horse, they having more horses than Whiskers had whiskers, many times over. So I got the idea that Whiskers must be somewhat nuts. And I thought no more about it right then.

It didn't come back into my mind until midnight, when the bronc' fighters came together at rodeo headquarters, in the blacksmith shop, to draw for the bronc's we would ride the next day. There were pretty near thirty riders entered this year, about a dozen from the big desert ranches around there. Old Whiskers Beck was there, and he seemed to know everybody—not only people around there, but people from all over. And he had worked it so that he was going to be an assistant arena director, on no pay, as is often the case with these old boys everybody knows.

So now it worked out that Whiskers Beck was the *hombre* who went down the list and gave numbers on little slips of paper to throw in a hat. Leaning over his shoulder, I saw him give Pain Killer number thirteen. When you go to a rodeo, take special notice of the horses numbered seven and eleven, and sometimes thirteen, because it is a kind of custom to give these special numbers to the worst bronc's.

Riders are always anxious to get seven or eleven in order to show off their stuff in a hard ride, but sometimes they are not so crazy to get number thirteen. Like in the case of Pain Killer, for instance.

Pain Killer finishing Bob Dennis had taken the starch out of some of the boys. These were good game boys, but they didn't look forward to being purposely tromped on, and there was hardly anybody there who really had any idea he could cowboy this horse. So they were quiet, not mentioning his reputation had grown until he pretty near overshadowed the rest of the show.

Ben Cord now came in kind of tipsy, crazier than ever, and he started right off by telling everybody in a bashful, quiet tone of voice, hardly any louder than the whistle on a steam engine, that, as sure as hell, he hoped he would draw Pain Killer—that was all *he* wanted out of this rodeo—and if ever he got hold of that horse, he was sure going to ride the tail off him, and show Pain Killer he had met up with his boss.

Mostly the riders didn't pay any attention to him, having seen tall talk before. But, you know, I think Ben Cord really wanted to get that horse. I don't believe he ever doubted for a moment that he could ride that horse right down into the ground. Those of us who had seen him ride, we knew better. From what Ben had showed so far, he couldn't have rode Pain Killer the best day of his life.

We waited around for time to draw, and pretty soon Ben went out, looking for another drink, and it happened that right then Whiskers Beck called up the riders to make their draws.

That drawing wasn't like any other drawing you ever saw. Mostly riders are anxious to see what they've got to ride on tomorrow, but this time, instead of trying to make out they weren't interested, the riders were trying to let on it wasn't their turn, and they didn't know the drawing had been called. And they were hanging back, just casual, not wanting to stick a hand in the hat and make the test. I believe the feeling was on everybody that Pain Killer, who had killed one boy today, was going to kill another before the twenty-four hours were out. You'd have thought there was a sidewinder in that hat.

I took a step forward, fixing to draw, and I'll be darned if that same superstitious feeling didn't come over me, and I stopped. I couldn't any more have gone up to stick my hand in that hat than if the devil had me by the hair. I rolled a cigarette, figuring to let just one number go by.

"We got to get going some way," Whiskers said. "You're all so backward, I'll draw for some of the riders that has stepped aside. I'll draw for Ben Cord." He stuck his hand in the hatful of numbers.

I don't know how many saw what I saw then. Sometimes I'm not dead sure I saw it myself. Only, it seemed to me, that something was palmed in Whiskers Beck's hand that went into the hat, and, as he drew his hand out again, I suddenly knew that the number he had brought out had never been in that hat to begin with.

"Ben Cord draws Pain Killer!"

Right away you could feel the whole works kind of draw a breath and ease down. Death was not in that hat any more. How many of them knew it never had been in that hat? I don't know. But whoever knew, there was none who begrudged Ben Cord the Pain Killer horse. Ben had asked for the killer, and he had got him, and he was welcome to him from them all.

Pretty soon I drew, and got just an ordinary bucker. I went on over to the dance hall and danced with a girl rider from down in the Great Bend country, three or four dances, and got in a fight with a calf roper who had figured to dance them dances himself, and I got disbarred from the dance floor for a little while.

So then I stood outside smoking, waiting for the bouncers to forget that I was a source of disturbance. I was thinking about Pain Killer and the boy he had just killed, and wondering if Ben Cord might get by with just a lay-up in a hospital. And while I stood there wondering over these things, here came Whiskers Beck.

Old Whiskers was quiet and casual, but there was a gleam in his eye so that I knew for some reason he was on the warpath and going strong.

"Gil," he said, "you've got to side-ride me."

"All right, Whiskers," I said.

We went off, and we sat on the tailboard of a horse truck.

"You know these Helmholtzes?" he began.

"Not personally," I said.

"You're lucky," he said. "They're crooked, and they're mean, and they're hard. This boy, Johnny Fraser, that Ben and me have been working for on the Tonto Rim, he's the whitest kid that ever stood up, yet they've got him tied in a sack. They're going to strip him clean as a steer horn, and they're going to take off him everything that Johnny's paw worked for and fought for all his life. If ever there was a shame in the West. . . ."

"It won't be the first time the Helmholtzes have picked the bones of a good outfit," I told him.

"The kid has made a good game fight," Whiskers said. "He's come so close to winning, the crack of a bull whip don't separate him from holding on to his own. But every friend he's got has had to help him, and they've helped him all they can. More than a hundred thousand dollars has gone pouring through this fight, and now I tell you . . . Gil, you wouldn't believe it. I can't hardly believe it myself. But if that boy could lay hands on just five thousand dollars more, it would see him through!"

I looked at Whiskers in the dark. There's men who go through all their lives getting nowhere, just playing easy-come, easy-go. But if one of these men takes a liking to you, he'll fight your fight right down to the last penny or last cartridge, doing for you what he never would have done for himself.

"The Helmholtz brothers have papers on the key water holes of Johnny's range . . . one in particular," Whiskers said. "If Johnny could raise five thousand dollars more, he could save that one hole, and it would be the turning point of the fight. But when he loses that hole, the bankers will go out from under him like quicksand, and he's through. Just five thousand dollars, in a fight that's seen a hundred thousand gone."

Whiskers Beck sounded as if he could fight or cry, either one, at the drop of a hat. I never seen a dead loyal old man more tied into another fellow's fight.

"At the last minute before I come here," he told me now, "Johnny scraped together fifteen hundred dollars. I got him to let me take those fifteen hundred dollars, as a last chance, to see if I could win the five thousand with this little fast pony of mine. Well, as you know, the way things stand here there's no winning any five thousand on that horse."

"It sure looks bad," I said.

"But there's one bet I can make with this fifteen hundred. And adding to that a hundred of my own and a hundred that I borrowed, I've placed twelve hundred through different fellers . . . every cent bet with the Helmholtzes. Some of it I got at three-to-one, some of it at two-to-one, some even. Now I want you to take the other five hundred and somehow fix it to bet it with the Helmholtzes, at any odds you can. And, by God, we'll make them Helmholtzes furnish the rope!"

"What is this bet?" I said.

"That Ben Cord will qualify on Pain Killer!"

"You're crazy!"

He didn't seem to hear me.

"Ben Cord come and begged me to fix it so he would ride Pain. Every rider in the contest was praying that some such fix would be made. When I talked to the judges, they told me go ahead, work it if I could. Gil, I fixed that draw to throw Pain Killer to Ben Cord."

Well, I already knew that. I asked him: "Does Ben know this? And about your bets?"

"He doesn't know anything about it. He asked for the horse, and he got him, and he's happy. God knows," said Whiskers, "if I was twenty years younger, I'd have thrown it to myself. But . . . Ben will have to make the ride for me. And he'll make the ride."

I've never seen a rodeo without some kind of shenanigan, but as old Whiskers told me about this one, a kind of cold chill ran down my back. It seemed like he was telling me he'd as good as killed Ben Cord.

Suddenly I realized that this old man had real guts, more guts than it ever would have taken to set out to make the ride himself. It's one thing to take your own life in your hands, and another to throw the job to some other kid. Riders will always pretend they would rather see the other fellow take the chance any day, but anybody that believed that is a fool.

And on top of that. . . .

"I'm betting every cent of Johnny's money," Whiskers said, "and all I can scrape together on my own, that Ben Cord will qualify on Pain."

For a minute I couldn't hardly believe him.

"Then," I said straight into his beard, "you're a damned old fool! You're going to look good, explaining to this kid boss of yours that Ben Cord is crippled or dead, and that you frittered away his money betting on the ride."

The night was cool, but Whiskers Beck mopped the perspiration off the top of his bald head. "I know," he said. "This is a tough box for me, Gil. But it's the only chance in the world here at the last minute to save Johnny's lay-out."

"And a fat chance that is," I told him. "I know Cord, and I know the horse. There's not a chance in a million that Ben comes through."

But now suddenly Whiskers Beck seemed to be sure of his ground. "The boy will ride," he said. "He'll ride, and he'll ride slick!"

"For maybe three, four jumps," I said.

Whiskers Beck shut his mouth and did not come back at me, and now I saw that he had some idea up his sleeve. I waited, but it did not come out. It took me quite a little work to find out just what Whiskers did have in mind. But finally he gave me the story, to get me to place the final bets.

"I picked that colt up off the range two years ago," he said, "this horse they call Pain Killer. He was three then. He was a hard colt to handle . . . impossible for most fellers, because he was one you couldn't force. But I took him gentle. Gil, I've been on the back of this horse, Pain Killer, without saddle or bridle!"

"You sure must be mixed up," I told him.

"He would have worked . . . for me," Whiskers insisted. He leaned close to me. "He'll work for me yet," he said.

"You figure . . . ?"

"I can take the hell out of that horse just with my voice," he said. "I'm riding pick-up tomorrow in that arena. I'll be at the chutes when Pain Killer is saddled. You'll see him take the saddle easy and steady for once, with just me growling at him through the bars. I'll be riding close as Ben comes out, as close as I can keep my horse to the bucker. I'll be talking to him like I always talked to him back there when he would work for me and for no other man. I used to say . . . come on, boy . . . come on, boy. . . . just like that, and that steadied him any day in his life."

Whiskers Beck had one of these deep kind of chesty voices when he sung out to a horse, the kind of voice some men have who can lift a horse over a fence, or hold him down, just by talking to him. This idea of his was something I had never heard of before, exactly. But as I listened to him, I was actually beginning to wonder if there could possibly be anything in this.

"He'll buck," Whiskers was saying. "He'll buck honest, and hard, but the edge will be off him, and the killer will be out of him. You'll see Ben Cord make a pretty ride."

I began thinking about a couple of other things I'd run into one place or another. I've seen more than one horse that would work for only one man. I've seen buckers that couldn't really come unwound if you kept shouting their name. Those things gave a kind of color to what Whiskers Beck said, so that I saw that maybe there was one long distance chance that the old man might be right. Not enough of a chance, though, so that I wanted to be mixed up in his losing his kid boss's money.

"Whiskers," I said, "you can't do it. I won't lay your bet."

He looked at a big fat turnip watch he had. It was so late that pretty soon it was going to be early, but the Helmholtzes and their like would be around for an hour yet.

"Come on," Whiskers said, "I'll show you I know what I'm doing."

We got hold of a little broke-down flivver and run the

mile out to the arena. There wasn't anybody around the bucking horse corrals, and we went over to where Pain Killer stood in that little small corral alone.

It was awful quiet there in the starlight. The calves for the roping had quit bawling and bedded down, and about all you could hear was sometimes a kind of shuffle of hoofs as some mean-headed bronc' laid his teeth into some other bronc' that had drifted too close. Pain Killer was standing quiet, and in the dark he looked half again as big as he should, and two times blacker than the night. As we came up to the bars, I could see his ears prick up against the sky, and he blew out a long, ugly sounding snort. That Pain Killer had a salt-pickled heart, if ever a horse had. Whiskers Beck crawled through the bars.

Pain Killer stood still, watching him. He was one of those killers that stands quiet, never making a move, until suddenly he moves all at once. Whiskers did not go toward him, but just stood a little out from the fence, his thumbs hooked in his big belt.

"Boy," said Whiskers Beck, in that deep, hoarse talking voice, "what's got into you?"

They stood looking at each other for maybe a minute. Pain Killer moved his hoofs and woofed an uneasy breath.

You couldn't see Whiskers's grin there in the dark, but I could tell by his voice that he grinned.

"Come here, boy," Whiskers said. "You ain't forgotten me. You ain't forgot me at all. Come over here."

My hair kind of raised, like is likely to happen if you are watching something that runs crosswise of the regular way things happen, and you have the feeling that something is almighty wrong, without just knowing what. For now Pain Killer took a slow kind of cautious step toward Whiskers Beck.

I suppose it took Whiskers four or five minutes to get that horse to come across the corral to him. But little by little Pain Killer came. Those killers have their bad days and good days, and sometimes you can handle them for months without their making a pass at you, but to judge by what had already happened that day I figured Pain Killer was in one of his bad streaks. I was figuring that any minute he might whirl and lash out, or else come high striking with his front hoof and reaching for a hold with his teeth.

Pain Killer came clear up to where Whiskers could touch him. Whiskers took him by the ear, kind of rough and easy-going, and whopped him on the neck with his big horny hand. For a while he stood there, talking to him, while Pain Killer stood quiet as a wooden horse and never made a move.

Finally Whiskers crawled back through the fence, and Pain came to the fence and stood, looking through the bars after him. I went over to the fence just for a test, and Pain snorted and whirled and went to the far side of the corral. I turned to Whiskers Beck.

"I'll place your bet," I said. "Maybe you know better what you're doing than I do, for all I know."

I took Whiskers Beck's money and bet it with Ron Helmholtz, getting two and a half to one that Ben would not qualify on Pain.

I was the third bronc' rider out of the chute the next day, and I qualified all right, making an ordinary ride on an ordinary bucking horse. But hardly anybody around there noticed, I hope, how close I come to slipping a stirrup, just through not having my mind on my work. Everything about that rodeo seemed the same as dozens of other rodeos I had worked in—the lay-out the same, the stock the same, and the people the same—but somehow there was something unnatural about the whole thing.

There was the flat twenty-acre arena, sending up little dusty heat waves in the sun. There was the grandstand full of people, and the double rows of cars parked all the way around the arena fence, and there was the tall chutes with the big broadside gates that the bronc's came out of, and riders roosting around careless on the part of the chutes that was not being used. The calves were bawling, and a loudspeaker was squawking up in the stand, and a rumbling noise came from the crowd whenever something happened—everything just like usual.

Yet somehow nothing seemed usual about it to me. Stronger than ever I had that superstitious feeling that Ben had met his come-uppance. The more I thought about it the surer I was that Ben could not ride Pain, and would not live to try it again if he was bucked down, and that all that stood between Ben and a bloody smashing under Pain Killer's hoofs was just a gamble on the voice of an old man.

It seemed like all day before Ben's number came up, but Pain Killer was thrown into the chute at last. I saw him come into the chute fighting, hating the close quarters. They had a bad time getting him headed into the chute, at all, and, when they got him in, he stopped halfway between Gate No. 1 and Gate No. 2, and wouldn't be driven and wouldn't be led. Somebody laid a quirt across him to drive him up in, and he came up on his hind legs and whirled, trying to get at the man, and came crashing down in the bottom of the chute, kicking four ways at once. They finally had to use a bull gad to ram him into place.

By this time Whiskers Beck, who had been filling in for a judge in the calf roping, got loose from his job and came loping across. Maybe he could have gotten Pain into the chute without so much row, but by this time he was gated in and ready to saddle.

Pain stood there making a low, ugly kind of groaning noise down in his chest. His eyes had gone as hard as glass, not scared or unhappy, or worried, but just plain hard and ready for fight. His ears were pricked forward, and he was waiting for the saddle now. And suddenly I knew that, if they would change their minds and turn that horse back in the corral, Pain would be disappointed, he was so plumb eager now for a chance at his man.

A couple of the handlers were easing Ben's saddle down onto Pain Killer's back, and Pain stood steady. I saw him shuck his shoulders to settle the saddle into place. He knew the game! And now Whiskers Beck dropped off his pony and came to the side of the chute by Pain's head.

I heard Whiskers talking kind of low and deep to Pain, as he had talked to him the night before.

"Easy, boy. Take your time now, boy. Ain't you ashamed of yourself?"

Pain turned quiet so suddenly that my hair raised again, seeing the way that old man's voice could work on that killer horse. A kind of marvel came over me as I thought for a minute that Whiskers Beck knew what he was doing, had known all the time, and could quiet that horse till he would maybe buck no more than a little calf.

Then I saw that something was wrong. Pain was not standing quiet and easy at all, but just as rigid as if he was made of stone. I spoke to Whiskers, holding my voice casual and low.

"Whiskers, look out. Take your hand off that gate and look out."

And before the words were out of my mouth, Pain let go.

Pain's wind exploded in his throat in a kind of cough. He

came on to his hind legs quick as a lion and twisted in the chute to smash out with both fore hoofs at where Whiskers stood. If Pain had caught Whiskers's hand with the edge of his hoofs, Whiskers would have lost his hand. As it was, the side of one of his pasterns caught Whiskers's hand against the board of the gate, and we found out afterward that right there two fingers broke.

Whiskers Beck turned gray. He didn't jump, but after a second he took a step back and looked at his hand, as if he couldn't believe his eyes. The saddle they were putting on was only half cinched, and, when this happened, it slid back and to the side, pretty near under Pain's belly, such as would make any other bucking horse go wild, but Pain paid it no mind. The handlers cussed and reached down and worked the saddle up into place again.

Whiskers Beck stepped up to the gate again. "Boy," he said, "what's got into you? You gone crazy, boy?"

I tell you it was like as if he dropped a match into powder. Pain squealed this time as he came up again, lashing out at Whiskers with everything he had till you'd think that he would either break a leg or smash that heavy chute. I had climbed up on the fence ten feet away, and the six-by-ten post I was sitting on shook as if you hit it with a ten-pound sledge.

As the dust cleared and Pain stood quiet again, Whiskers spoke to Pain once more, but his voice was kind of wondering now, and very scared.

"Boy," he said, "why, boy. . . ."

This time Pain didn't blow up, but he measured the distance and rammed his head between the bars, trying to get at Whiskers with his teeth.

The handler who was trying to get the saddle on Pain stood up on the side of the chute and shoved his hat on to the back of his head, cussing.

"Get that old brush-faced pelican away from here," he said, "or get somebody else to screw this saddle down! Don't you know no better than to stir up a horse a man is trying to cinch?"

Whiskers turned away and walked a little way along the fence, and kind of slid down the fence to sit in the dust. Looking at him, I knew what was in his mind. He knew now that his scheme had blown up in his face and worked out so that he had just about as good as killed Ben Cord.

I dropped off the fence to squat beside him.

"It's all right, Whiskers," I said. "You done the best you could."

"Good God," Whiskers said, so you could hardly hear him. "Good God in heaven!"

"He may ride him," I said.

"The man don't live," Whiskers said in a dead voice, "that can ride Pain the way he is today."

I opened my mouth to say something, but I shut it again, I was so dead sure that Whiskers Beck was right.

Whiskers turned to me. "Listen," he said, whispering, "stop Ben . . . get hold of him before he climbs that chute. You've got to. . . ."

"There's no use talking to Ben," I said.

"Talk to him, hell! Call him the worst names you can think of, and then bring up your right clear from the heel of your boot and knock him cold! It's the only. . . ."

I jumped up, not waiting to hear the rest. I hadn't ever interfered with anybody's ride before, but all of a sudden I was willing to interfere now. I don't know if I would have tackled it on Ben's account alone. For though my hunch kept riding me that he was going to die, that's the bronc' rider's choice when he asks for a horse, and he has the right to make it alone. But here was this old man who had studied it all out, not for his own sake but for somebody else. If things went on for a minute more, he was going to spend what was left of his life blaming himself, and never able to get out of his mind the picture of a thousand pounds of crazy squalling horse driving hoofs down into something bloody in the dust. I was going to do what Whiskers wanted, and try to crack Ben down before he could ride.

But now I saw that I was too late. It only takes a second or two to jerk tight the cinch and make fast, and the rider slides into the saddle and his helper, straddling the chute, heaves upward with his back, trying to cut the bronc' in two with the flank strap.

All that only takes a couple of seconds, and the quicker after that you come out of the chute the less likely you are to be down in the bottom of it with a thrashing horse. They had gone through those motions very fast, once Whiskers had turned away. I saw that Ben was in the saddle, and the boy who had stood over him to heave upward on the bucking strap was already off the gate.

Ben shouted: "Damn it, will you swing that gate?"

The loudspeakers had already announced four or five times that Ben Cord was about to come out on Pain Killer. There was a second or two of complete silence now, as the boy handling the gate snatched loose the rope and swung the gate clear. That gate swung open right in my face, and I like to got stampeded over as that big black cyclone of a horse came out.

I made a move toward where Whiskers's horse had stood, its reins down to hold it, but Whiskers had already flipped the reins over its head and was vaulting into the saddle without using the stirrup. So I turned back to watch how many jumps poor Ben would ride in maybe the last ride of his life.

I had seen Pain buck before. I knew that horse. I knew both sides of him—top side and bottom side—for I had seen the one from the saddle and the other from the ground, with his hoofs coming down on me in that second when Bill Daly crashed his horse into the killer and made him miss. And nobody knew better than I knew that this horse had everything.

He had the double pound that is caused by a horse sucking his back from under you just before he bumps it again and hits the ground, so that, instead of just the plain shock of jump and hit, it is as if he hauled off and struck upward at you with a thousand pounds. He had a sun-fishing twist, and he could come down out of it so straight upon his forelegs that at least once in his life he had gone clean over in a somersault, smashing the rider under the cantle of the saddle so that he never walked again.

He could twist and turn on his side so low that it seemed your stirrup swept the ground, plumb careless of how he would come down if he fell. But most of all he had such a terrific crazy power to him as I have never felt in any horse, and once his rider was unbalanced, Pain never jumped back under him again. After that it was just a question of whether your pick-up men could get in to ward him off in time as he whirled and came back, striking down.

I said I knew that horse. I mean I thought I knew him. For I never knew Pain or any other horse to turn on as Pain turned on now. Maybe it was the blood in his nose from having got his man the day before. Maybe it was the voice of Whiskers Beck somehow tangling up and working backward in the dizzy meanness that passed for Pain's brain. I know that Pain never fought like he did that day, and never did again.

On the first jump, as Pain came out of the chute, Ben's spurs swung high, raking him down the side of his neck, and Pain bawled and blew up. He took two long leaping jumps to gather speed, then went up in the air and came down with such a full hard stop, straight up on his forelegs, that he was able to make his next jump really backward. Pain whirled, leaning so deep on his side that I thought he was down, then again two more of the hardest backward jumps I ever saw.

And still Ben was riding him—not just staying with him, but raking him crazily from mane to saddle blanket on every jump. It seemed to me that Ben was not using his legs to keep him on that bronc' at all, but just somehow balancing in the seat of the saddle, swinging both stirrups wild and free as he scratched the horse. That is the test of a bronc' rider—not how long he can stay, but how high he can scratch.

I swear, time and time again I saw daylight under Ben's spurs—daylight between his boots and the top of Pain's neck. Somehow, for no reason, Ben Cord was making the ride of his life, riding better than he knew how, better than he could possibly ride. Cowboys who had seen a thousand bronc' riders were staring glassy-eyed. Only the ignorant ones, who had only seen a few, maybe failed to realize that you could follow the bronc's for a hundred years and maybe not see such a ride again.

The killer bawled and put everything he had—more than any horse has a right to have—in maybe five more short, high, sun-fishing bucks, and still Ben's spurs swung high, though he had long ago passed the first three bucks where you really have to scratch the neck to qualify. Now Pain Killer, crazy wild that the man still stayed, threw himself, turning into the air, and came down any old way, no hoofs on the ground. I thought for a second it was a somersault, but somehow he twisted and came on the side of his neck, then down on his side.

There was Ben, clear of the stirrup that was smashed under the horse, standing over Pain Killer. And he was in the saddle again as the black horse sprang up.

At last the whistle blew. I don't know for sure, but I'll bet that whistle should have been blown long before, only the timekeeper had forgot where he was or what he was supposed to do, watching that ride. Whiskers Beck crowded in as Pain still went down the field in those crooked sunfishing jumps. Whiskers got an arm about Ben and dragged him clear of Pain Killer, and Ben squirmed up behind Whiskers on the other horse.

I stood there and rolled a cigarette. It was only beginning to dawn on me that Ben had made the ride that Whiskers had bet he would make. What got into Ben, that he was able to do that? I don't know. He didn't know about the bet with the Helmholtz brothers, let alone anything about Whiskers's shenanigan to make it a possible ride. He didn't know anything about any of that. I don't believe, as he rode, he even realized that he was riding for prize money, but just rode for the love of riding a tough one, riding the tail right off of a killer horse.

What do you suppose Ben said as they set him down at the chutes? That wild Indian, that crazy kid, he just said: "What's the matter . . . ain't you got any tough hosses here?"

He didn't know yet he had saved Johnny Fraser's brand.

I didn't see Whiskers Beck until that night, when our trails crossed while he and I both were hunting around town for another drink.

"Well, Whiskers," I said, "I guess you won your bet."

"Yes, I guess I won the bet."

"The only thing now is to get your money."

"I got the money," he said.

"And this saves Johnny's lay-out?"

"Well, I guess it as good as saves his lay-out."

"It sure will be a big moment for you," I said, "when you ride in there and break the news to Johnny that you've laid hands on the dough."

Whiskers Beck shook his head. Some code of his own sure had him in a stranglehold. "Everything I did worked out wrong," he said. "What it amounted to, I threw away Johnny's money. And not only that, I threw away Ben Cord's life. Yes, his life, you hear me? All the smart things I rigged up went to hell in a cloud of dust, and nothing would have been saved out of it, except for the hellfire riding of a wild, crazy, half Indian kid. Gil, I'm an old man and a washout, and this is too much for me."

"Just the same," I said, "you got plenty guts . . . more than me, more than Ben himself. And you'll find you've got a home for life, back in the Tonto!"

Whiskers shook his head again. "I'm sending the money to Johnny."

"Say . . . you mean you aren't going back to. . . ."

"I'm hitting the trail the opposite way," Whiskers said.

He turned and walked off into the dark, walking just as steady as if he had not downed enough whisky to kill two men. I never saw him again.

Sentenced to Swing

"Daw-gone it," protested Brian Duffy plaintively. "Daw-gone it! I was afeared of this exact thing. Here's the Malloon Desert . . ."—his short fringe of white beard quivered with emotion—"with no more than one head of people to every eight hundred square miles. But let a man lay hands on a rich sample of ore, and the rumor runs from one end of the Malloon to the other quicker'n a greased pig on skates."

His partner, Peculiar Shirt Smith, set in on him savagely: "And what about this deed signed Aloysius MacGinnis? What about it? Is it forged like they say? Dast you write your name, right here on this table top, so we can see for ourselves whose handwritin' tacked on that name?"

Brian Duffy raised aged blue eyes humbly, and looked briefly at each of the men who stood over him. Although there were but four of them, including his own partner, the little cabin at the head of the Three Burros shaft seemed packed with people. Besides Peculiar Shirt Smith, there were those two silent and ugly-looking strangers, the short man with the washed-out green eyes, and the dark-faced *hombre* who looked as if he had less sense than thirst for trouble. Worst of all, there was the wiry man whose graying hair still showed a trace of red—the one who had dropped a bombshell on the partners by announcing himself as Aloysius MacGinnis, original discoverer, and sole owner, of the long-abandoned Three Burros mine.

"If you think I'm not MacGinnis," said the last, "you can take it into court. I can raise up a hundred men, I betcha, right here in the Malloon, that remember me . . . Aloysius MacGinnis."

"Yeah, I recognize you myself," Duffy admitted painfully. "I guess it's you, all right."

"And if you still claim I signed this shaft over to you, I'm willing to write my name down, and then you write it yourself, and we'll see plain who planked it onto that deed. I'll tell you straight out, Santy Claus, I never saw you before in my life. Here . . . gimme a pencil. . . ."

"Ain't any need, to speak of," said Duffy sorrowfully. "I'll own up to it, Aloysius. 'Twas me rigged up the deed."

Peculiar Shirt Smith turned a pair of furiously popping eyes upon his aged partner. "You cold-decked me, then!" he yelled at Duffy. "You got me to come in with you and put up the stake on a dirty, sidewinding. . . ."

"It's a harsh way to put it," said Duffy humbly. "I meant it all for your own good, Peculiar. I was virtually certain that MacGinnis dynamited a good vein, when he upped stakes and blew, twelve years back. And I couldn't've opened the shaft alone at my age, and broke. So, you being so offish, and making so many objections, I just made that up about me having a deed to the old mine. I needed a stake, and a right honest and husky young man. . . ."

"I knew there'd be some catch to it!" said Peculiar Shirt bitterly.

". . . so that night I wrote out the deed myself," Duffy finished lamely.

"I don't want any trouble with you boys," said MacGinnis. "But if it's trouble you want, I've come prepared for it."

"Yeah . . . I've observed you so done," sighed Duffy. "Well, easy come, easy go. . . . I ain't beat. I kin find me another."

The next morning Duffy and his partner, Peculiar Shirt Smith, rode away over the Casket Range.

"Tough break for the old corkscrew," MacGinnis admitted when they were gone. "Well, that's the last we'll hear of *him*."

It was the last, for all of three days.

On the morning of the fourth day three riders appeared in the notch of the Casket Range. Two of them were Duffy and Peculiar Shirt, but the third was a leathery, one-eyed, old party, who carried his sheriff's star in his pocket.

When MacGinnis and his two homely friends had been called out of the shaft, the hand of MacGinnis made a slight motion toward his holster, but he reconsidered in time, for there were rifles in the hands of Peculiar Shirt and Duffy, and the one-eyed sheriff had some small reputation of his own.

"I'll have to take all three of you boys, I'm afraid," the sheriff announced. "The rope's waited for you a long time, Aloysius, but I reckon it'll still hold. I guess it must have slipped your mind about the trial, where you was convicted of killing both them Benton boys!"

MacGinnis considered while his face grew pale. "No, I was just hoping it would be brushed over like . . . it's been so long. Can't say I forgot, exactly."

"Neither," said the sheriff, "has the law."

"Well," MacGinnis said, "I guess you got me on conspiracy to defraud. But that's all you got me on. I'm not Aloysius MacGinnis. My name's Wilbur H. Harkness. That being the case, I may as well go with you, I guess."

"I guess you had," said the sheriff. "The other two *hombres*, too, on general principles. Saddle, you jiggers, I got to get back!"

"Well, for cat's sake!" said Peculiar Shirt when they had gone. "*Can* he prove he ain't MacGinnis?"

"I'm virtually certain," said Duffy, "that he kin. Fact is I wouldn't've called in the law on him if I hadn't believed he could worm out. It was funny about those killings. You see, MacGinnis really killed the Benton boys in self-defense. Only the evidence made it look bad, and he was sentenced to swing, if he hadn't broken loose and sloped. No, I wouldn't have give him away, if I'd really thought it was him, not for all the gold in the Malloon. It wouldn't've been right."

"But how did you know it *wasn't* MacGinnis? You said your own self you recognized him."

"Well, you know yourself, Peculiar, lots of fellers find cause to take unto themselves fresh names . . . such as Smith, for instance."

"Well, of all the fool. . . . Say, you tellin' me you just *guessed* he wasn't MacGinnis, because lots of fellers use the wrong name? Well, of all the darned. . . ."

"Not exactly," admitted Duffy. "We'll just take back this shaft, Mister Shirt Smith, by right of uncontested re-openry."

"But how did you know it wasn't him?" Peculiar Shirt insisted.

Duffy slowly surveyed his partner from head to foot, and back again, with a mild but thorough eye.

"Well," he said at last, "I was virtually certain, on *that* point. You see I happen to be Aloysius MacGinnis myself."

The Fourth Man

"I ain't to be discouraged by no such a small thing," averred Whiskers Beck, the aged, white-bearded patriarch of the Triangle R cowpunchers. "I've set my mind on goin' to this Bar C dance an' gen'ral shindy in soo-preme comfort an' style. An' I aim to do so."

"Not disputin' with yuh," said Squirty Wallace, the wiry little top hand, "that it would be real comfortin' for you an' me an' Dixie to play stud in the back of the chuck wagon while somebody else drives, but I'm afeared the deal is off. That flunky says he won't drive for us for no consideration. An' just to make sure we wouldn't make him, he's went to work an' rode off, leavin' us flat."

"Think o' havin' a low, suspicious attitude like that," Whiskers marveled. "He must 'a' read my mind. But I ain't beat yet. Now, if you two boys would jest take turns drivin' the team, neither one would have to drive hardly half the way. An' meantime, the other two of us could be playin' cards, plumb peaceful an' free o' dust. That's my idee of a real. . . ."

"Well, not much!" declared Dixie Kane, the young bronc' peeler. "An' I should think not! Me an' Squirty does the drivin' an' collects up all the dust six horses can kick up while you sets all pretty under canvas, huh? Well, me, I'll just fork the one horse."

"Me, too," agreed Squirty Wallace. "We may get a few

shovels o' dust sifted down the back of our neck, but we won't get the whole Loop Hole Road throwed in our face by the bucket!"

Whiskers Beck rolled mournful eyes at the log buildings of the Triangle R home camp.

"Well," he said, "I got one plan left. I sure ain't honin' to be jiggled into a heavy sweat over twenty miles o' road. I'd druther use brains. Now how's this? We'll take the old spring buckboard. We'll hook on that team o' bays, jest the two hosses. The buckboard is so light that they won't have no trouble, not even in Dead Woman's Pass. Soon's we get that team started down the road, we'll jest forget about 'em. No one will need to drive. That team is as good at holdin' the road as any I ever seen. Step along purty, too. Bet it won't take 'em two hours fer the twenty mile."

"How'll a buckboard keep us out o' the dust?" Squirty wanted to know.

"We'll rig up one o' those old tents we used in that Cork Mountain camp that time. Soon's we get the team headed down the road, we'll lash the flies shut, an' there we'll be, inside with our lantern an' our cool drinks an' a deck o' cards an' the back end open for fresh air an'. . . ."

"Darn if that don't sound purty good," admitted Dixie Kane.

"Looks like every time the team takes a notion to stop an' eat, we'll have to unlash the flies," objected Squirty, running a hand through his rusty hair. " 'T that rate we'd get to the Bar C along about the early part o' September."

"Aw, poo-bah," scoffed Whiskers. "I can crack the side o' the tent with my quirt, so's it's the livin', spittin' imitation of a whip crackin'. I can even imitate the w'istle o' the lash, like this . . . *swrreet* . . . *pop!* That'll make any cayuse spraddle out an' get a move on!"

Squirty Wallace's thoughtfully wrinkled face relaxed into a grin. "If I don't think you've got the right idee!" he conceded at last. "This cow country has gone on too long 'thout the comforts an' refinements o' home. What's the use o' bein' us if yuh can't do nothin'?"

"That's what I say," agreed Whiskers heartily. "An' leave me tell yuh somethin' else." He drew them confidentially about him. "It's goin' to rain."

"Blah," said Squirty, "you make me sick. I dunno if I want to go ridin' with a crazy man or not!"

"I wisht it would rain," declared Dixie Kane wholeheartedly.

"Ain't that original?" Squirty burst into laughter. "Oncommon. The only folks that has thought that previous, up to the time you suggested it, was all the cattlemen an' all the hands an' all the saddle stock an' one hunerd percent o' the critters an' most o' the picket pins an' all o' the. . . ."

"I wisht it would rain in sheets," pursued Dixie. "Just downright pour. I'm sick o' wadin' knee-deep in dust, everywhere. The wet cows gives dust for milk. The steers has to walk with they heads throwed back to keep from walkin' on they tongues. I wisht it would rain ontil. . . ."

"Take a look over the shoulder o' Mount Saleratus to the west there," urged Whiskers. "What do yuh see?"

"Nothin," said the two 'punchers in chorus.

"Rain," declared Whiskers, squinting his old blue eyes into the west. "Not more'n two hundred miles off, an' comin' to beat the cards!"

"Whiskers is gettin' old," said Squirty to Dixie confidentially. "Beginnin' to show it, too."

"I'll jest lay yuh even money . . . ," began Whiskers.

The cook's horn brought the dispute to an abrupt end.

* * * * *

The clear, dry twilight, almost as light as midday, but without the glare of the desert sun, was upon them as they got their odd vehicle under way. It was seven o'clock in the evening. Already many of the cowboys had ridden out, resplendent in the best clothes they could muster, on their way to the dance at the Bar C. An unexpected amount of work involved in the construction of their special car had delayed the three inventors. But they were well pleased with their work and confident of arriving at the Bar C by nine o'clock.

Unlimited ingenuity combined with a minimum amount of labor had gone into the construction of the "parlor cyar" designed by Whiskers Beck. Poles of various uneven lengths had been lashed together in a framework adapted to support the grayed canvas of the tent. Due to the stretchy quality of its rope trusses, this superstructure swayed slightly, but, nonetheless, it at once showed itself to be surprisingly roadworthy on the whole.

Within, several war bags stuffed with blankets and other blankets spread on the floor of the buckboard provided couches where the three might recline as they played.

A lantern, well anchored, was suspended midway between floorboards and ridge pole to provide light as needed. A bucket, half full of sloshing water, acted as a refrigerator for several bottles, for, as Whiskers pointed out—"In this country a snake may r'ar up an' bite a man any minute."—and they wished to be prepared for any contingency. No comfort was lacking, and if the buckboard was somewhat jouncy and teetery of movement, at least it in no way simulated the harsh pounding encountered in the saddle of a trotting horse.

A few belated 'punchers swept past on their mounts,

raking them with jeers, ribaldry, and mocking laughter. But the three, reclining in dustless comfort, grinned with the satisfaction of men who enjoy the fruit of their brains and know when they are well off.

The reins, entering their moving tent through a crack beneath the tightly lashed forward flies, pulsated slightly with the jogging movement of the invisible horses. The reins showed a slight tendency to sneak away through the crack, and Whiskers, after some thought, finally tied them about his right leg. By seven-thirty the dusk had deepened materially, and they lighted the lantern and had a drink.

Dixie Kane, settling back on the blankets to examine the cards that Squirty had dealt, heaved a huge sigh of contentment. "When I think," he said, "o' the rest o' the boys, painfully poundin' leather in the heat an' dust in a desper'te effort to get where they're goin', I could pretty near cry!"

"Yeah," said Squirty. "Ain't it painful t'watch the pit'able struggles of the ignor'nt?"

"Only one thing is lackin' to make m'happiness complete," said Dixie. "I wisht it would rain!"

"You jest keep on wishin'," said Whiskers, "an' mebbe so you'll get your boots rained full yet tonight."

Another half hour passed—a half hour of luxury, peace, and restful, if somewhat joggly, locomotion.

Squirty Wallace was dealing a particularly interesting hand of stud poker. Dixie Kane, with aces, back to back, on the first round, calmly drew out a ten dollar bill, and dropped it in the middle of the triangle they formed on the bouncing floor of the buckboard. Ordinarily he would not have dared spoil a good hand by such a high initial bet, but Squirty and Whiskers both had deuces showing, and deuces were wild.

Solemn, with sarcastic remarks about ten dollar bets

made "under the gun," the other two matched Dixie's ten dollars in kind. Three more cards were dealt. Dixie drew a king. Whiskers a second deuce.

"Boys," said Squirty, "somethin' tells me I got the winnin' hand right here in this deck." Slowly he drew off the top card, very deliberately began to turn it over.

Poof! That vicious first puff of wind clapped into the traveling tent with almost the force of an explosion. A swirl of dust came with it, leaping into their eyes, and the lantern trembled, flickered, and all but died. In the failing light, through the whirl of dust, they saw three hands of cards take wings and fly out of the wagon.

"Damn," said Squirty, "there goes the three best hands. . . . My God! The tens went with 'em!"

Frantically they searched the tent. The currency was nowhere.

"Dixie! Quick!" yelled Squirty Wallace.

He sprang for the opening at the back just as the team leaped ahead, startled by the commotion. Squirty, his footing jerked out from under him, took a gigantic plunging step into space and landed prone in the dust with a mighty *plop*.

"Stop the wagon!" howled Dixie Kane.

"Whoa!" yelled Whiskers, hauling desperately upon the reins.

Dixie Kane, hastening after, tripped over a rope, and Squirty was consoled by a second *whop* in the dust that told him Dixie had followed suit. Together they scrambled up and dashed, cursing, back along the dusty road.

A sullen darkness had descended with ominous swiftness. The air seemed darker than the land, giving the rough landscape that they had entered a singular ghostly appearance. Great swirling dust devils, revolving, solid-looking columns twenty feet tall raced along the road, looking like pale, phosphorescent specters. One of these plunged upon them as if to seize the hurrying men, and for an instant they were lost in a blinding, choking swirl.

Nothing was to be seen of cards or greenbacks. Even as they frantically peered this way and that the darkness thickened until they could not longer see each other. The rushing dust devils, too, disappeared, but the men could hear them howling and hissing about them with a noise like the rushing of myriad ghostly feet on sand. The wind now began to howl among the scraggly pine of the foothills they were traversing.

"Back to the wagon, Dixie!" yelled Squirty. "Them moneys is plumb relapsed into memory!" Then, as no answer came: "Dixie! Dixie! Where are yuh?"

No answer. Squirty turned and dashed for the covered wagon. The horses started with a jerk as Squirty tumbled in.

"Where's Dixie?" demanded Whiskers.

"I dunno!" yelled Squirty above the mounting voice of the wind. "Wait! Stop! Hold on!"

Whiskers somehow brought the nervous team to a stop. Both together, they hallooed long and loud. It seemed to them that the wind would not possibly let their voices travel beyond the walls of their swaying, wind-racked tent. But, after a moment, a faint answering hail was heard. It came from ahead, far down the road.

In a moment or two Dixie arrived and tumbled in among them.

"I guess I run past, when I made for this here parlor cyar," he explained sheepishly.

The team hurried on as Whiskers relaxed the reins. Great thudding drops began to batter down upon the walls of the tent, singly and distinctly at first, each drop a separate blow, and then in an increasing volley that swept into a crescendo roar, filling the lurching tent with dizzy sound. A mighty thunderbolt crashed to the earth, illuminating the walls of the canvas with a blaze of white light. They could feel the shock, and an acrid smell of sulphur filled the tent.

"Gosh," said Dixie Kane. "Be they shootin' at us, or was that just plain careless?"

The whirling growl of raindrops now was varied with the impact of heavy water, bucketfuls at a time. The rain was literally coming down in sheets. Another terrific crash of thunder, the impact of sound coming simultaneously with the blazing white flash, striking the earth near them. Then another and another, until the lightning was so continuous that a man could have read a newspaper by its glare if anyone would have felt like reading in the terrific bedlam of screaming wind and mountain-smashing thunder.

A rope had given way, so that one side of the tent sagged. The pocket of canvas at once filled with water, tubs of it. Suddenly, just as the thunder roared again, the canvas split, drenching Dixie Kane with the full volume of water and whipping cupfuls of cold rain into the faces of the other two. A damp hysterical spluttering of oaths came from Dixie as he emerged from his first paralyzed assumption that he had been struck by lightning.

"Dixie wished it would rain," said Squirty Wallace.

The racking, swaying buckboard, plunging along behind the frightened, galloping horses, was now traversing the narrow road leading through the rough country of Dead Woman's Pass. The canvas circumscribed their vision, but the downward dives and brief, almost perpendicular, climbs told them that they were traveling over tricky ground at a breakneck pace.

"Ain't . . . the lantern . . . holdin' out . . . good?" yelled Whiskers in brief breaks in the thunder.

As he spoke, a terrific screech of wind burst through the rent canvas, puffing out the kerosene firefly and wrenching it from its moorings. Dixie Kane seemed to be the leading goat this night for it was upon Dixie's hat that the flailing lantern smashed. Thereafter, for the remainder of the night, all who came close to Dixie noticed a strong odor of kerosene.

"Who done that?" they heard the bronc' peeler demanding in a dazed, aggrieved voice.

A lurch of the wagon flung Squirty upon Whiskers.

"Looks like rain!" he shouted into Whiskers's ear.

"Damned if it don't," Whiskers returned. Then: "I shouldn't've reminded Ol' Master about that lantern. He shore took me up!"

A smother of ropes and canvas swept down to muffle his words. For half a minute the three 'punchers fought to free themselves from the tangle of wet canvas, blankets, ropes, arms, and legs. The tent had given it up. The buckboard wrenched and hurtled, flinging them this way and that as they struggled to win free of the all-enveloping wreckage. More than one set of knuckles received a tattoo of blows from the whizzing spokes of the wheels.

Then, just as suddenly as the canvas had descended, another crescendo blast of the incessant wind plucked it away, sending the tent whistling and whirling into the unknown. It was now revealed to them that they were racing drunkenly along a dangerous part of the road. On their left, the mountain climbed vertically above them, a steep of forest, tangled brush, and jutting ledges. On their right, the world fell away abruptly into the valley, so that a pebble flipped from the buckboard would have fallen into the tops of tall pines below.

All this they learned in one blinding, crashing flash of lightning, in which they saw the thrashing treetops dimly through rain thicker than fog. For an instant they glimpsed a pair of blankets, winging across the valley, flapping madly, like great crazy crows. The full force of the wind was now upon them, almost tearing the men off the buckboard. Whiskers swore afterward that the buckboard was sailing like a kite behind the stampeding horses. It touched the ground, he said, only four times in three miles to his positive knowledge.

The rain was now pouring down upon them so solidly that it was difficult for them to catch their breath. Frantically they clutched at cracks in the flooring to hold themselves on with one hand each. Each cupped his other hand over his nose and mouth, that he might gulp a little of the drowning air. Their hats went and the handkerchief from around Whiskers's neck. Dixie Kane's shirt cracked down the back with the force of the wind, and the rags fluttered and snapped about him, gesticulating in a mad dance.

"How heavy the dew is tonight," gasped Squirty Wallace, but the water drowned his voice.

The buckboard was now plunging downgrade at a terrific rate, and Whiskers, taking his hand from his nose, clutched the reins in a heroic effort to hold the horses back. His labor steadied the team somewhat, but could not check their speed.

A steep incline rose ahead of them. At that moment a series of lightning flashes blazed about them, and through the sheeting rain they saw that a tree was down across the road at the top of the rise. With one accord, Dixie and Squirty seized the reins near Whiskers's hands and pulled. The team came to a sliding stop, their hoofs in the brush of the tree.

A few moments of utter darkness followed the series of flashes. Through the roar of the descending water they heard Whiskers yelling: "Get out an' . . . lead team . . . unhook . . . lift buckboard."

Dixie leaped down from the buckboard and instantly discovered that he had leaped in the wrong place. Down and down he shot, with no ground under him, until a greasy clay bank brought his fall to an end in a harmless, scooping swoop. Before he could pick himself up, there was a hissing sound above him, and another man came rocketing down the slide, catching Dixie in the ribs with both feet as he slid to a stop. Evidently Squirty Wallace had made the same mistake.

"Catch hold my belt!" yelled Squirty into Dixie's ear.

No man was more swiftly master of an unexpected situation than this bowlegged little top hand.

Dixie groped in the dark, found Squirty's belt, and crawled after Squirty as the latter began struggling up the almost perpendicular ascent. Dixie now became aware that someone was hanging onto his belt. A dazed checking up of his count proved to him that there were evidently three of them involved in the climb where he had thought there were but two. Assuming that Whiskers had also negotiated the flying descent, he said nothing in complaint of the unfairly heavy drag upon him as they climbed.

Gripping roots, vines, stems of grass, anything, they crawled their way up the ascent, twisting about to dig the high heels of their boots into the face of the mountain. Eventually, half drowned, with their clothes full of sand and their boots brimming with water, they reached the top.

At this point Dixie became slightly confused. As they floundered over the last overhanging edge on to the road and gained their feet, a flash of lightning revealed Whiskers standing erect in the downpour at the heads of the horses.

"How did he get there so quick?" Dixie marveled. And then: "Can there be four of us here, I wonder?"

There was no time for idle speculation or the meticulous counting of noses. Whiskers had found a way through the débris of the fallen tree, through which the horses might be led. Squirty unhooked the buckboard, and Whiskers led the skittering, frightened horses through the blockade. Then, with superhuman efforts, Dixie and Squirty set about getting the buckboard through.

It is a curious thing, significant of the characters of these men, that not then or at any other time did they think of turning back. The idea did not so much as occur to them. They had started for a dance; they would keep going, and get there sometime.

By a gigantic labor of heaving, hauling, twisting, and shouldering, working in alternate pitchy darkness and blinding flashes of blue light, they got the buckboard through—almost. Somehow, in the tangle of tree, the hind wheels wedged and stuck. Whiskers was signaling frantically for haste. Abruptly they gave up getting the buckboard through by hand, and hooked the horses. Either the horses would jerk the buckboard free or they would not. They thought it worth the try.

As they hooked the horses to the buckboard, Dixie thought he saw a tall figure standing motionless a little apart, spectral in the midst of the down-pouring water. He shot another glance in its direction in the inert flash, but it had gone.

Whiskers now came tumbling back from the horses' heads, frantically sorting out the reins. He was yelling something in their ears: "Waterspout . . . Dead Woman's

Gully . . . flood . . . make it across . . . race for it . . . for God's sake let's go!"

His idea swept over them as a revelation. Down ahead, just before the climb through Dead Woman's Pass, lay the ravine called Dead Woman's Gully. Perhaps even now a raging torrent fifteen feet deep was boiling through the cut. Even if it were fordable at the moment, any instant might see a solid wall of water storming down the gully, smashing all before it, turning a dry wash into a foaming rapids in which nothing could live.

"Let 'er buck!" yelled Squirty, tumbling onto the buckboard any old way, Dixie after him.

Whiskers, perched just back of the horses' dripping tails, paused only to take a turn of the reins around his leg for surety, raised his quirt with a yell.

There was a diversion.

"Stick up yer hands!" roared a hard-edged voice, plainly understandable even in the steady roar of the sheeting rain. An icy wet muzzle pressed under Whiskers's ear, and another against the side of Squirty's neck. By the same flash of light that had guided the intruder's guns, they saw a long, evil face, singularly sinister in appearance in the blue light and disgustingly close to their own. They saw the water running off the stranger's mustache in streams. Then darkness, an awful moment of doubt and suspense.

The wet sounding *crack* they heard then must have been the cut of Whiskers's quirt upon the streaming rump of the off horse. A wrench, a leap of the buckboard under them, a crashing noise, a three-foot drop, the thunder of receding hoofs, and Dixie and Squirty realized that the front wheels and axle of the buckboard had parted company with the rest. A vast blaze of white light showed them the fleeing horses and Whiskers, sitting on the small of his back in the mud, but traveling rapidly after the horses, by virtue of the reins he had wrapped about his leg.

It showed them something else: the stranger, floundering on his back on the slippery incline of the buckboard, his guns waving at the heavens like ominous antennae of a great insect. With one accord the two cowboys leaped upon him.

Guns went off, so close that their ears rang with the explosions. Bony knees met them with jabbing blows. The butt of a revolver raked the side of Dixie's head. At one point in the struggle, the lightning revealed to them that Squirty was trying to break Dixie's arm, while Dixie was flailing punches at Squirty's eye. Over and over they rolled—the three—off the buckboard onto the road, where they wallowed and sputtered, fighting in the deep mud. Then off the road and down a twenty-five foot drop into the clay bank from which they had so recently emerged.

That ended it. The cowboys had somehow managed to light on top, and the fight was knocked out of the obnoxious stranger.

"Goin' t' keep this feller . . . souvenir!" shouted Squirty, sticking the gun that did not get lost into his belt. "Have sheriff . . . make dog meat!"

They hauled the limply crawling enemy up the bluff and onto the road by the ears, as they might have dragged a bawling calf. Grimly they started down the road, their captive between them, looking for the wreck of Whiskers and the team. Thus, hurrying, they crashed into a wheel of the buckboard. In the next flash they discovered Whiskers, unhurt. He was trying to turn the team about to come after them.

Squirty Wallace now found a rope end still trailing from the axle, and he tied it in a hard loop around the captive's neck.

"Hang on to that axle or hang on the run!" was his brief advice.

Whiskers asked no questions. As soon as this was done, they heard Whiskers yell. "Gra-a-ab the axle, boys! We'll race . . . Dead Woman's Gully . . . or bust! Hi-yah!"

Gripping the reins and the axle with one hand and his quirt with the other, the astonishing old man lashed at the team. Dixie and Squirty made a flying dive at the axle, and just made it as the team and the remains of the buckboard plunged downgrade into the drenched dark. Dragging, floundering, sometimes gaining their feet to run a few monstrous hurtling steps before going down again, they clung to the axle.

The water poured down from above more fiercely than ever, and the lightning roared almost continuously. Wind and water seemed to tear the breath from their mouths. Rocks in the leaping road beneath them beat and ripped at their knees, and in their faces splattered a ceaseless stream of mud from the horses' hoofs. But they hung on!

Below them the gully moaned, its floor filled already with the water from the local downfall, a rushing, swirling muddiness perhaps waist-deep. But from above came an ominous, thundering roar, the accumulated water from the mountains above, coming down the gully in a solid wall. The horses heard it and slid to a trembling stop.

"Don't try it!" shouted Squirty above the voice of the storm. "For God's sake hold that team!"

"We can make it!" yelled Whiskers, his quirt slashing.

The trembling horses, their ribs heaving, their eyes starting from their heads, shrank from the punishing lash, yet hesitated for an instant with hunched backs and downstretched noses on the brink of the gully. Then they plunged into the water below. Thrashing, struggling, half drowned, the horses plunging ahead in a wild panic, they fought their way toward the opposite bank.

It seemed to Dixie Kane that he had never seen a gully so interminably wide before. Half dragged, half floated, almost torn away by the rush of the current, the men clung to that slender axle.

"We've made it!" shouted Whiskers hoarsely.

Just then the diapasons of the storm suddenly swelled to a terrific roar, multiplied and multiplied again as if an ocean were catapulting upon them. With their powerful backs straining with the fear of death, their flying hoofs gashing the slippery bank, the team went up the wall of the gulch like squirrels. A mighty weight of water, its front a heaving wall almost triple the height of a man, hurled itself down the gully in a deafening tumult.

The crest of the wave struck Dixie Kane's trailing leg with an impact as solid as that of a club, and the grip of the water wrenched away his boot. The horses rushed on up the grade beyond danger. One by one the men dropped off, to lie gasping for air. All except the stranger who, because of the rope about his neck, was still in hazard of being summarily "hung on the run." The team, freed of the deadly, dragging weight, staggered to a level bit of ground and stopped.

The men looked back and, by the blue flare of the lightning, saw thirty feet of the bank they had left collapse into the seething flood in the gulch. From wall to wall the draw was filled with a bulging wrath of water in which nothing could live. They saw a great hundred and twenty foot pine, its roots heaving skyward like clutching, imploring hands, swept tumbling down the torrent, as helpless in the teeth of the flood as a bit of shingle, or a man.

★ ★ ★ ★ ★

Inside the big new barn of the Bar C, festivities had been proceeding undampened by the storm. Decorations were few, but there was plenty of kerosene light, and the crowd on the floor, while comprised chiefly of men, was colorful enough to make up.

Enthroned in a manger rack in one corner was the orchestra. It consisted of a fiddle, played with spirit by a little, bald old man with a nutcracker face; a rather small accordion, energetically wheezed by a red-nosed miner with an oversize mustache; a huge banjo, thrummed mightily by a tousled, black-headed giant, bearded to the eyes; and a complete set of drums, operated with more enthusiasm than technique by a young cowboy with a copper-riveted face.

As an auxiliary to this official orchestra, a corps of volunteer mouth organ experts, ranging in number from two to a dozen, according to whim, clustered in front of the orchestral manger, contributing their best. When the measures raced with turbulent abandon, the harmonicas were operated with both hands, while their owners bent and swayed, beating time with a thunderous stamping of feet.

There was no sheet music. The little, bald old man with the fiddle led off with each piece, and the others trailed in. In case some of them didn't know just what the fiddle was playing, they improvised as best they could, the strength of their instruments undaunted by any slight vagueness as to what was being played. And if there were occasional discords as a result of these misunderstandings, no one noticed them.

An uproarious atmosphere of merriment pervaded the crowd of fourscore people of plains and mountains who danced. The liberal scattering of flasks that were whipped out at the close of each dance, and the hogshead of beer that welcomed all comers in the corner, had already done a good deal toward relaxing restraint. The advent of the desperately needed rain, bringing financial salvation to many and new life to thousands of head of stock, did the rest. With the music at its height, the men whooped and cheered, and the building shook with the rhythmic trampling of feet.

While the fewness of the women was a source of regret, it was not permitted to retard the dancing. Smooth-shaven cowboys with clicking heels and bearded miners who danced like bears reeled and whirled together in the waltz. Those who could not waltz did not hold back. Many a bearded, merry-eyed couple could be seen performing steps that appeared to be half ring-around-the-rosy and half wrestling match.

The thunder and roar of the storm outside—the insistent wail of the orchestra, bravely combating the hammer of the downpour on the roof—the rhythmic *thud* of feet—the bright dresses of the women and the untamed colors of the men's shirts and neckerchiefs—enthusiastic whoops and cowboys' yells—the kaleidoscopic whirl of movement—laughing tanned faces—twinkling eyes above brushy beards and the gay, flushed faces of the girls. These things made the barn dance a bacchanal, a riot of vigorous spirit.

Big Shocky McCoy stepped up onto a keg to call a square dance. His powerful voice boomed clearly through the tumult of the rain, and the orchestra struck up once more at his command. A slight confusion occurred at the start, for the fiddler struck off with "Old Zip Coon," whereas the remainder of the orchestra had expected to play "Pop Goes the Weasel," and failed to note the change.

A brief, unmusical struggle ensued, each laboring musician looking at his fellows with vaguely puzzled, accusing eyes. Then the majority won, and the fiddler was dragged into "Pop Goes the Weasel" against his will. Half a dozen squares were formed; the rest of the crowd, lining the sides of the floor, clapping their hands in time with the music.

Swaying his shoulders, Shocky roared the dance calls: "Form a squar' with the four right hands, back to the left, an' ever'body swing! Allemande left, and watch yer step, an' gents all turn, an' promenade! Face yer pardners! Jine right hands! Grab yer girl, an' ever'body swing! Quarter a whirl! Fifty cents! Seventy-five! An' a dollar a whirl, whirl yer girl, why doncha!"

The Spring River sheriff, a man with jovial red cheek bones and a jauntily upturned mustache, now remembered that he had forgot something. He strode to the door, the door representing the flattest available surface in a building chiefly of logs and poles, and dragged a large, damp handbill from his pocket. He also produced tacks and proceeded to affix the black and yellow sheet to the inside of the door.

The orchestra stopped opportunely, and the sheriff seized the chance offered by the slight pause between the whoops of applause and the resuming music to make his announcement.

"Leave me call yer 'tention," he roared, "leave me call yer 'tention to this here . . . !" He flung up an outstretched arm to point at the poster. At this moment the door was unlatched from the outside and, swung violently inward by the wind, it cracked the sheriff on the elbow. "What the . . . ?" he began.

Into the room filed Whiskers Beck, Squirty Wallace, and Dixie Kane. That is to say, the three that filed in knew themselves to be such. No one else recognized them. Drenched, their boots squirting water at every step, mud-colored all over, their clothing torn in shreds, the newcomers baffled identification by even their closest bunkmates. The faces of the streaming three were masked with gooey mud through which rivulets of water had carved clean streaks, giving the masks a peculiar wavy, stripy appearance. From these masks their eyes looked out like three pairs of hard-fried eggs. One of the three appeared to have a beard, decorated tastefully with some intertwined sticks and leaves. But no one could be sure.

A hush fell upon the throng, broken only by the drumming of the subsiding rain on the shakes above. For a moment the fourscore stared at the three, and the three stared at the fourscore. Then the leader of the three—he with the twiggy beard—pointed a thumb half over his shoulder at one of the other mud-masked figures.

"Dixie was just wishin' it would rain," he solemnly intoned.

Pandemonium broke loose. Shrieks and howls of laughter shook the roof, drowning out the sound of the rain. 'Punchers reeled, roaring with laughter, into each other's arms, beat their nearest friends with hard hands, and sank, doubled convulsively, to the floor. Hats sailed into the air. An unsuspected gun went off, potting the roof, and an instant stream of water was admitted by the wounded shingles. The first cupful of water, with divine justice, went down the gun-toter's neck, cooling his ardor somewhat.

While this uproar was going on, the three had stood limply, without facial expression. There is no expression to mud. But suddenly he of the dripping beard set eyes upon the sheriff's posted handbill and galvanized into life.

"You want Saragossa Pete, do yuh?" he yelled above the shrieks of the laughter-racked mob.

"Right," replied the laughing sheriff.

"Well, we got him right here!"

At this the sheriff from Spring River became swiftly sober and alert. "What?"

"We got him! How much does that reward read?"

"Three thousand . . . dollars . . . reward!" yelled the sheriff as impressively as he could. "For mail robbery, shootin' up o' seven men, rustlin' o' cattle, robbery on the highway, blowin' o' the Hogjaw bank, settin' fire to the. . . ."

"Well, here he is!" yelled Whiskers excitedly. "I know his pan, an' I seen it tonight by lightnin'." He seized upon the hindmost member of the three, and hauled the bedraggled fellow forward. "This is him."

The sheriff promptly thrust a gun into the shirtless stomach of the man thus presented. At this the news that something extraordinary was going on at the door spread over the assemblage like ripples in a pool, and all fell silent to listen and watch.

"Wait!" protested the man who confronted the sheriff's gun. "I ain't him. It's me!"

"Damned if it ain't!" Whiskers admitted. "My mistake, Dixie. Reel in that rope!"

Dixie Kane, he of the missing boot, carried the end of a rope that extended out the door into the night. He now threw his weight upon it. In response to this peremptory summons a huge, shadowy figure appeared in the doorway. At first the crowd thought that a horse was being led in, but instead a fourth man, in every way like the mud-disguised three, lurched in weakly, led by the rope knotted about his neck. The arms of this latest entry were bound behind his back, and his feet were hobbled so that only short, teetering steps were possible.

In spite of these handicaps, the prisoner was seen to make a game attempt to bite through the rope that led him, an attempt that was ended by a harsh command from Dixie Kane.

The sheriff ripped off his own handkerchief and thrust it outside into the drip of the eaves. It came back soaking wet, and he used it to get some of the worst mud off the face of the prisoner. "It's him for sure!" he exulted. "I know by the scar over his right eye!"

While the sheriff had washed the prisoner's face, Dixie, Squirty, and Whiskers had followed out the idea by rinsing and rubbing some of the thickest clay off of their own. They were now recognizable to those who knew them well.

"Well, if it ain't Whiskers!" declared the sheriff. "An' Squirty! An' Dixie Kane! All from the Triangle R. How come yuh to get this feller?"

"Well," Squirty began, "I knowed there was somethin' phony about him soon's he stuck that gun in my ear, so we thought. . . ."

"We went after him," Whiskers interrupted loudly, drowning Squirty out.

The sheriff swiftly shoved the reeling prisoner ahead of him into the room, his gun at the man's back. He held up his free hand to silence the general buzz of excitement.

"Listen!" he yelled, and they did. "Whiskers Beck, Squirty Wallace, and Dixie Kane, all o' the Triangle R, has run down an' captured alive this here Saragossa Pete, the same feller that shot his way through three posses. They took him with the' bare hands, follerin' a long chase through this storm! Yuh can see for yourselves they ain't got guns!"

There was a moment of silence except for the steadily decreasing hum of the rain while this sunk in.

"Three thousand dollars reward is comin' to these boys," the sheriff concluded, "an' I'm gonna see that they get it!"

A great cheer went up, continuing, with whoops and yells and leaps into the air, for many minutes. Flasks were thrust into the hands of the three, and they were mauled and thumped by many hands. Then swiftly they were swept up onto the shoulders of six brawny men. Shocky McCoy leaped onto his keg.

"All form for th' gran'march!" he bellowed.

The fiddler struck up "Hail to the Chief," and the orchestra crashed in.

The three dripping 'punchers from the Triangle R, each with a flask in each hand and a thousand dollars gold in prospect, were carried triumphantly at the head of the grand march on the shoulders of shouting men.

"How was the rain, Dixie?" Whiskers yelled over his shoulder.

"Rain?" Dixie Kane shouted back. "Where?"

The Fiddle in the Storm

It was already past midnight when, through the blinding run of the snow, Jud Hyatt pushed against the sod wall of the stable and knew that he was home. Hyatt's sense of direction was equal to any in the territory, but in the black sear of the blizzard a man could lose track of anything that he could not reach out and touch, so that he was both surprised and immeasurably relieved that he had made it, after all.

Dismounting, he groped along the wall to the door, kicked it free of the ice that jammed it, and led his pony in. He unsaddled, slinging his hull into a corner as if he were never going to need it any more, groped for a fork, and shook down a bait of hay. Then he drew a deep breath, plunged out into the blizzard again, and ran, stumbling, toward the house.

The blast of the norther ripped the breath from his lungs. It seemed to fill all space with a vast thunder and the snarl of dry ice particles rushing horizontally across iron-crusted plains. So thick was the night that he was unable to see a faint patch of lighted window until he barged into the massive log wall. Then he was inside, in stove heat and lamplight at last.

Jean Campbell was standing by the big wood range in the little kitchen. Her red-gold hair was the single vivid spot of color in the room. She was staring at Jud Hyatt as if he were a ghost.

Jud Hyatt felt curiously stunned and dazed, now that his struggle with the night was so suddenly at an end. His head was still ringing with the blast of the norther as he heard himself say: "Hello . . . why, what's the matter?"

"Jud, are you crazy?" Her low voice was furious. "We thought you'd hole up in the southwest storm soddy . . . haven't you any sense at all?"

"Well, shucks, honey, I thought I'd better come on in."

Jean Campbell gave a little whimper and ran into his arms, disregarding the mass of snow needles that had pinned themselves into his coat and were now melting with the heat of the stove. She clung to him, and the quick tears upon her lashes were warm and wet against his frosted cheek.

"Jud, if I'd known you were riding back against the blow, I'd have died."

Late though it was, nobody at the Bar Cross had turned in. A hum of talk that had been going on in the big main room had stopped as the blast of cold air through the house announced Jud's arrival. Now there were people crowding to the kitchen door, their eyes startled, like Jean's.

Abe Campbell, for whom Jud Hyatt rode, was the first to press into the kitchen, his close-clipped beard bristling like a handful of shingle nails. "Good Lord, Jud!" There were nearly a dozen people gathered here tonight, and because they were all cow folks, range people, they knew what manner of death walked in those black blizzards, in which a man could lose himself and die while trying to go from his house to his barn. That a man should have attempted to travel in such a night—and have made his destination—was an incredible thing.

Mrs. Campbell, a billowing motherly woman with sober

eyes, seemed most surprised of all. "Jud, are you all right? I declare I don't know what gets into you youngsters. It's got so I can't draw a peaceable breath any more with a storm up and you boys not in. Froze anything?"

"Shucks, no. I just thought I'd better. . . ."

Mrs. Campbell said crossly: "Don't be a fool, Jud! Everybody get out of here . . . all of you. How am I going to feed this boy with the whole passel of you underfoot?" She began to make a great clatter of pans.

As the people who had pushed into the kitchen shuffled out again, Abe Campbell kicked shut the battened door, and instantly Jud Hyatt turned upon his boss.

"Luther Kendricks get here?"

"Sure he got here! He said he was coming, didn't he? What he says he'll do, he does. He's in there now."

For a moment Jud stared dumbly at his boss, then he turned away and began pulling off his coat.

For six months Abe Campbell had been trying to get old Luther Kendricks to come here to discuss putting a block of money into the Silver Bow cattle. Old Kendricks had half the money in the territory, and, having made it in cattle, he kept it there.

To invest in the Silver Bow was to invest in Abe Campbell purely, for the range encompassed but three brands, and it was Campbell who had gone on the notes of the other two, and held them up. By himself he could hold them up no more, or even save himself any longer in the face of the bad years. And now that Luther Kendricks had come at last, he had arrived just in time to see the Silver Bow getting away from them, stripped and scoured clean by such a blizzard as few of them could remember.

"Where'd you come in from, Jud?" Campbell demanded.

"From the Hat Crick bluffs."

Campbell exploded at Hyatt. "Why didn't you say so? Are they there? Don't stand there like a ninny! Are they under the bluffs? Are they there?"

"No," said Jud Hyatt heavily. "There's no cows under the Hat Crick bluffs."

Campbell looked as if he could not believe his ears. "You're crazy! They've got to be there! Where else can they stand against the norther? They've got to be there . . . you hear me?"

"I was there before dark. I doubt if there's a hundred head between Wagon Bend and the Sauk Breaks."

For several moments more Abe Campbell stared at the cowboy without change of expression, but, when he spoke again, his voice was curiously low and the stiffening was out of it.

"All night," he said, "I've thought of Hat Crick as our one best bet. If they drift before it, hell can't save 'em, Jud."

It's the fool white-face strain, Jud Hyatt thought. *We should have kept more longhorn blood.*

Mrs. Campbell was slamming things around the stove. Already the little cook room was filling with a grateful smell of frying beef. She said: "There's still a chance that a big part of them can stand to it in the Silver Bow bottoms."

"I touched the Silver Bow at the upper bend," Hyatt said, "and the wind's whamming through there to turn 'em wrong side out. There's a big bunch of stock in there, about half of 'em down. I tailed up near forty head before it come dark. They wouldn't hardly move, but only just jerk their horns and bawl. Looks to me like they're good as gone . . . those I saw."

Old Campbell's bristly jaw was set. "We'll come through this yet," he said stubbornly. "In a couple hours more this storm should turn."

"And if," Mrs. Campbell said, "it doesn't turn?"

"By God," said old Abe Campbell, "she's got to turn!" He went stomping out into the main room, slamming the door.

Mrs. Campbell set out hot beef and potatoes for Jud Hyatt, and Jean sat on the other side of the home-made table as he ate. While Jean was in sight, nothing else ever actually existed for Jud, and now the ringing was going out of his head, and the black punishing hours of his cross-wind fight were beginning to fall away behind him. Sometimes she made him feel as if he wanted to fight and smash things, and other times as if nothing was worthwhile but to take her protectively in his arms and tell her how beloved she was, what a bright, warm decoration she was to the gaunt prairies.

In the three years in which his fortunes had been linked with those of Abe Campbell, she had become the center of his whole existence. He could ride a lonely week and hear her voice under the wind all the way. At night by his fire he could see her hair bright in the glowing smoke, and her smile teasing him from the flame.

"Jud, do you think . . . ?"

"A few of the leatherheads might get through. Not many, I guess."

Jean's words sprang from her passionately. "If this isn't a cattle country, in heaven's name, what is it?"

"It's grand cattle country," Hyatt said, still believing. "This come at an unhandy time, that's all."

"And now . . . what's ahead?"

"Your father's the best cattleman in the north, Jean.

He'll make his stake again."

"I mean . . . you and me."

Jud Hyatt shrugged. He had had five hundred head of his own running with Campbell's Bar Cross stock, until the blizzard struck. "I better slope down Texas way, and see to a job. Pretty soon I'll build me a new stake. Someday, if the big company brands don't grab up all the range. . . ." He saw the tears come into her eyes, and he reached across the table to grip her hand. "We've still got a chance. If the storm turns, a lot of stock may pull through in the willow breaks. Meantime, we've got to play up to Kendricks. By God, we'll find a way out of this yet! Who all's in there?"

"Nearly everybody in the Silver Bow. All of the Bassetts . . . Charline and her brothers, and Grandpappy Noah . . . and Lief Norgaard's two girls, and Curt Webb, who rides for him . . . and, of course, Rees Butler."

"Lief Norgaard . . . where's he?"

"He went down just before dark to cut the south drift fence so the cattle won't be piled up there, if they drift. Sigrid and Helga came on here, with Curt Webb."

"You'd better come on in if you've et," Mrs. Campbell said.

"We're coming."

As they stood up, Jud stepped around the table, caught Jean in his arms, and forced a hard unexpected kiss against her cheek bone. For an instant she turned her face upward and pressed her lips against the corner of his mouth before she pushed him away.

The main room was a big one, for this house had been built for a barn—only, the barn had proved so much more comfortable than the soddy that the Bar Cross people had moved into it. Campbell had meant it to shelter horse rakes and mowers, when he got squared around. The huge stove at one end, red-hot as it was, could heat only a little space around itself tonight.

The storm was searching out every last crevice, so that within the house a hundred faint icy breezes kept moving about from unexpected angles. The blizzard bawled like a world in torment, wrenching at the sturdy logs. The night was an enormity, an illimitable blackness filled with unworldly sound and intense, rushing cold. Something was going on out there that was terrible in its immensity, yet specific and deadly in its meaning here.

The people gathered here were cow folks, all of them, men who had put the best of their lives into opening a range, and youngsters born to the saddle. They sat soberly, silent for the most part, not trying to conceal that they were waiting—waiting for the barely possible turn of the storm that would give them a little hope.

Jud Hyatt grinned and spoke to his friends, then walked across to shake hands with Luther Kendricks, who he had never seen before. As Hyatt shook hands with the visitor, he was comparing him with his own boss, wondering if Campbell, the cowman whose herds were withering under the stroke of the storm, could sway this other Westerner, who could raise a million dollars, or five million, if he had the mind.

Kendricks's long, smooth-shaved face had the heavy folds that age puts into only the thickest and toughest skin; his smile, rueful and grim, was of the mouth alone. The eyes were old past smiling, it seemed, but hard as rock drills. Hyatt judged that nothing was to be hoped for from this man if morning showed the cattle dead.

Hyatt heard Ma Campbell say: "It doesn't seem to be slacking much . . . it even seems to be getting worse." And Abe Campbell's dogged answer: "She's bound to turn."

Then silence again.

They sat so stoically impassive under the continuing disaster that they seemed to him more like Indians than like his friends. Then he ran up the ladder into the loft and brought his fiddle down. He sat down between Ma Campbell and Jean.

"Jud Hyatt," said Jean, "don't you dare play that thing! Because, if you do, I know I'm going to cry."

"Me, too, maybe," said Ma Campbell. "He can make that saw-box bawl like a baby!"

Jud began tuning the strings. "This outfit looks like a ring of coyotes fixing to sing gloom over last year's buffalo bones. What kind of a sorry outfit will Kendricks think this is?"

"You'll only make everybody feel worse, I bet."

Jud grunted, and the fiddle began to sing, a shrill, thin voice under the vast growl of the blizzard. The tone of that fiddle was slightly nasal, and it was fingered none too accurately, but Jud bowed it with a careless abandon.

Soddy back of Silver Bow. . . .

Hyatt saw Luther Kendricks's head come up slowly, like the head of a weary old dog. Even to Kendricks that song must have been familiar, although the version Jud was singing was a localized one that he had made himself.

And often by the Silver Bow,
When all the West was dry,
The wind picked up the Silver Bow
And threw it in your eye. . . .

Those who had danced to Hyatt's fiddle had never heard

"Silver Bow Soddy" as they heard it now, against the realization that the range had beaten them at last. Even the indomitable youth of Jud Hyatt could not bar from his mind the fact that spring and the new grass on the range would probably find neither Jean nor himself in the Silver Bow, and that their paths would thenceforth be separated, perhaps forever.

And I suppose I'll never
See Bow Silver
Silver back o' soddy.
Silver back o' Silver,
Any time ever,
Any time ever. . . .

That was not the effect Hyatt had started out to get at all, but, slash away as he might at the thumping beat, he couldn't get any other. He turned his eyes to Jean in a wordless appeal. For several moments they looked at each other. "All right," Jean said at last, "I'll try." Jud switched his tune to the "Irish Washerwoman."

"Stand to your partners!"

Jean Campbell sprang up, caught Curt Webb by the wrists, and pulled him to his feet. Nobody else moved, and those two, just those two alone, danced something that was partly square and partly improvisation.

Curt Webb danced constrainedly, his powerful shoulders looking hulking and awkward in his black coat. But the slim, quick-spirited Jean danced like a brightening flame. Her red-glowing hair tossed loose about the black silk muffler at her throat, and she clicked the puncheon floor with the high heels of boots that were the envy of every cowhand in the Silver Bow.

A ramping, a stamping, an Irish man . . .
A swaggering, swaggering Irish man.

Presently some of the others joined them—Johnny Bassett and Sigrid Norgaard, Rees Butler and Charline Bassett.

Sigrid Norgaard was tall and very lovely, but it was Charline Bassett, that wild, hard-riding girl who had been reared in the saddle, who was able to help Jean pick up the spirits of them all.

Steve Bassett, at seventeen the best roper in the Silver Bow, got Helga Norgaard to dance with him as Jud went into "Powder River Buck."

Big Sioux buck, rattling a rattle . . .
Ladies lope forward, gents bow low!
Counted fifty coups in imaginary battle . . .
Gents all forward and around you go!

And now Grandpap Noah Bassett, a little bald-headed man with a face like a carved walnut shell, got himself a pair of axe handles and began a syncopated drumming on a pack box. The fiddle, astonishingly, began to hold its own against the roar of the norther. Jean Campbell, whose spirit was sister to flame, was dancing as Jud had never seen her dance, and the flash of her defiance was spreading to the others. There was something fantastic, but glorious, too, in the vitality of those youngsters, dancing under the storm.

Stamping out a war dance, pounding on a drum . . .
Opposite partners, double swing!
Whipped the very devil out of Old Man Rum . . .
Step right back and swing 'em again!

The pack-box drum ranted and hammered; the fiddle was singing its heart out. Pouring himself into his work, Jud Hyatt did not realize that he played an hour, and a second hour. He played until his fiddle got hold of them all, and picked them up, and carried them along. He played until even old Abe Campbell got up and danced with Ma Campbell. At last, when Jud looked at Luther Kendricks again, he saw that the old man's heavy face was relaxed, and the drill-hard eyes that had seemed unable to smile were smiling.

But even with Jean Campbell to help him, he could not carry them forever. Presently, when he saw that Jean was tiring, he found himself thinking of another dance they had had in the Silver Bow, three years before, in celebration of the arrival of Abe Campbell's first big white-face herd. Once, while they were bringing that herd up from the old Nations, Jud had ridden thirty-six hours foodless and thirsty, back trailing a little bunch of eight or nine that had got off from them some place. All that, years of it—and now unless the storm turned. . . .

The tune he was playing came to end, and Jud Hyatt was straining his ears to hear if the changing timbre of the norther's roar suggested a swing of the wind. No one spoke; all the rest were listening, too. The tension of waiting for that improbable change of wind had become unbearable. Suddenly Campbell got up and lighted a lantern.

"Abe, you're not . . . ?"

"I'm going out to look at the thermometer, and the wind."

Luther Kendricks spoke for the first time in an hour. "It's been sounding to me as if she might be turning."

"She had to turn!" There was a strange steady surety in Abe Campbell's voice. It was as if he believed that his own faith, bred of bitter necessity, could itself have turned the storm.

Jud Hyatt went out with Abe Campbell. The thermometer hung in front of the house, but because the house faced the north—the Silver Bow was on that side—they didn't dare open the big front door to let the storm blast in. They went out the back way and fought their way around the house, the lantern sheltered under Abe's sheepskin coat.

At first, as they came out on the south side, Jud thought the wind was as savage as before. At the corner the full force of the norther struck him bodily backward, snatching the breath from his throat. He struggled on along the wall of the house and gained the front. There was no thermometer to be found upon the north wall. When Abe Campbell couldn't find it with his mittened hands, he half uncovered the lantern, and in the moment before the wind blasted out the shielded light they saw that the wind had taken their thermometer downcountry with the lost stock.

Just outside the door of the ranch house, in about the place where the thermometer should have been, stood a black hulk—the carcass of some lone steer that had barged, blind and driven, against the logs. There it had stood, resting, with the points of its horns in the wood, and there it had died on its feet, stiffening in the whip of the storm.

Abe Campbell was trying to shout something in Jud's ear, and, although the words were lost, Jud managed to guess what Abe was trying to say, and a sudden stir of hope jerked up his head. For a moment or two he stood trying to compare the set and power of the norther with his memory of it three hours before. The fury of the norther was terrible yet, but it seemed to him that its force had lessened.

Abe Campbell, obviously of the same opinion, was pounding him with a sledge-like fist. If their judgment was correct, it meant that the power of the norther was broken. They groped for each other in the bitter cold, and shook hands, then Campbell led the way back around the house at a run.

When they had got the kitchen door shut again, Hyatt saw that the fighting light had come back into Abe's eyes. "She's broke," Campbell said. "She's turned and done!"

Jud Hyatt wasn't sure yet. "That steer," he said, "you recognized that steer that's dead in front?"

"No!"

"That's that old longhorn leader."

Abe Campbell knew what animal he meant. The old steer was a Texan; he had been a marker in their herds for a long time. "Maybe so."

They went back into the main room. "She's broke!" Campbell told them all. "She's playing out, and we'll have the ponies under saddle before noon!"

For a moment the others were silent, as if they had been dazed by the punishing of the storm. "It comes too late," Rees Butler said at last. "These many hours, the bulk of the herds have been stiff and down."

Old Abe turned on him furiously. "Down, hell! These cattle know every foot of the Silver Bow ranges. If they was new on the range, they'd be finished. But they're not new. There isn't a gulch nor a bank nor a willow windbreak that isn't sheltering its cows tonight!"

"Seems funny," Jud said, "that there's none under the Hat Crick bluffs."

"I can't explain that," his boss admitted. "But I tell you they know their range. There'll be losses, sure, but they'll be little losses that we'll never feel. We'll find the bulk of them standing safe in the Sauk Breaks!"

There was a silence. "Well," said Grandpap Bassett, without conviction, "they'd better be in the Sauk Breaks."

The house so creaked and complained, with everything loose about it taking on a voice of its own, that they did not hear a fumbling rattle at the kitchen door, or guess that any living thing was there, until a cold blast ripped through the house. Abe Campbell, moving quickly to shut the door against the wind, let out a great shout as he reached the kitchen.

"Lief! In God's name. . . ."

As Abe got the door shut, they all crowded into the kitchen to see for the second time that night a man who had undertaken to travel in the storm.

Lief Norgaard, not so tall as his daughters, was squarely and massively built, with great powerful hands that could pick up a horse by the hocks and set him over into the traces. He moved stiffly and clumsily now, staggered by exhaustion. His feet were bundles, for he had cut his saddle blanket in two and wrapped the halves about his boots.

He said hoarsely: "My pony give down out here within the half mile. Good thing you had the door open, minute ago. I'd have missed the house, for sure."

Sigrid put her arms around her father's neck, beginning to cry, but he gently put her away and began unwrapping himself. There were great clots of ice in his mustache and in his chestnut beard.

"Man, man," said Abe Campbell, "what ails you, to come through the storm?"

"I was down at the south fence, cutting wire, like you know . . . so's the cattle could drift through, in place of piling up on the fence to die. I holed up in the storm shack for a while, but the roof blew free and a wall come in, and I couldn't keep any fire there. So I come on, following the fence." His voice was weary, dead. "We're finished, Abe. Cutting the wire was a waste of time."

"Finished? You mean . . . ?"

"The big end of the cattle is already dead. Along the drift line they're piled up by the hundred. Half of 'em was dead, some on their feet, some down, even before I come with the wire cutters. Even them that was alive couldn't be quirted on."

Abe Campbell said: "I thought the Sauk Breaks. . . ."

Lief Norgaard flared up at him, his voice rising with a bitter rebellion. "Sauk Breaks, hell! All you'll find in the Sauk Breaks is them that died there! We don't own fifty head of live cattle to the brand. I've been there, and I've seen, and I know! In all the world before there's never been such a cruel night."

They stood and looked at him, nobody having anything to say. This, then, was the end, utter and final. The end to even Abe Campbell's stubborn faith. Now the storm could turn and break and die, or never come—it would all be the same to the people here.

At last, after many moments, Ma Campbell turned automatically to the stove, getting coffee for Lief, and something for him to eat. Abe Campbell moved slowly toward the main room.

The others mostly followed Abe. They moved silently, like people struck dumb and stupid by the finishing off of hope.

Suddenly Jean Campbell broke. She clung to Jud Hyatt, tears running down her cheeks. "It can't be true . . . it can't! We mustn't let it! You're the only thing I've ever wanted in all. . . ."

Abe Campbell called to her from the door. "Jean," he said in a hard voice.

She stiffened, shook her head as if to clear her eyes, and wiped the tears from her face. As she turned to follow her father out of the kitchen, she was composed and her head was up.

Jud Hyatt walked after her, aimlessly. He looked about him, thinking idly that this was the last time he would see these people together here. He was noticing casual, pointless things. Abe Campbell's gun rack. Stock saddles piled in the corner. Jean's hair, like a sullen flame against the silver-gray of the peeled logs.

Something else was behind Jean, behind the log wall. As if he were looking through the solid logs, he remembered that black hulk that stood there—the frozen leader steer, grotesque evidence of the savagery of the night.

Suddenly Jud Hyatt angered, somehow caught between his desire for the girl and the pressure of that frozen steer that stood horn-locked against the outer wall. Driven, he caught up his fiddle again and gave a long wildcat wail as he dragged the bow across the strings. Everybody looked at him, startled, and he began to grin, a little crazily, out of the white heat of his anger. Then abruptly he began to play again.

Jud had a face that was always grinning, and anger could not wipe that grin off. It put a kind of craziness into the grin, making him look like a man who could be shot away bit by bit, and still keep coming back for more, not knowing he was licked even when he was dead. That same crazy grinning recklessness had, in different ways, its counterpart in them all, only temporarily subdued. They were of several races, but of one frontier. A group of people who had no common ancestry or tradition, but something else that could bring them closer together than that—a concealed courage, a resistance to misfortune that marked them as the material of a new breed—the breed that was called American, once.

"Stand to your partners!"

For a little longer they stood uncertain. Then Curt Webb began to laugh, a wild roaring laugh that ended in a hazing cowboy yell. Curt looked about him and saw that Jean was laughing, too, unsteadily. He caught her up with an arm about her waist, and spun on his heel, swinging the girl clear off the floor.

Jud Hyatt set up a long yell answering Curt's, above the squalling of the fiddle, above the continued voice of the storm. "To hell with it!" he shouted. "What's couple of thousand cows?" It was strange to hear that from Jud Hyatt, who had given all that was in him to save the herds. "Leave 'em all die! Leave 'em all blow over the hill!"

Abruptly something broke, there in that log house under the storm. Charline Bassett pulled Rees out into the middle and made him dance, and Steve caught up Sigrid Norgaard. Abe and Ma Campbell joined them. Suddenly Jean Campbell dropped Curt Webb, ran across to Luther Kendricks, and made him dance with her. Curt Webb began shouting the dance calls.

> **Form a square with the four right hands . . .**
> **Back to the left . . .**

The thing that had broken in that big dim room was the grip of disaster. Strangely, abruptly, it had cracked away, unable to hold them any longer, now that the last of their hope was gone. The fiddle ripped and sawed, and, although it was but a thin voice under the diapason of the tormented prairie, its song was the soul of something else that was the master of disaster.

Big Tom Bowlin, hunting hard for trouble!
Big Tom Bowlin, howling out a song!
Big Tom Bowlin, shouting and a-shooting.
Stampeding half the country as he rides along. . . .

After all, those old square dances had something. They were dances full of swing and drive, dances of motion and liberated energy. In those people was the vitality of a thousand miles of prairie soil—the soil that had supported ten million buffalo and, now that the buffalo were gone, did not know what to do with all that vitality, but was destined to support a nation. The bitter lash of disaster could not beat back the upwelling thrust of that waiting power. "Big Tom Bowlin," as they danced it now, diverted into a defiance, the very energy that the ebbing storm had spent to destroy them.

Presently, as they danced, something changed within the lamp-lit room, so that somehow it became friendly and cheerful. That barn was home, the buffalo robes on the walls were luxury, and even the chilling drafts were reminders that here was haven from the ruthless black wrath of the night.

A faint gray light was coming up over the edge of the prairie as Abe Campbell brought out a bottle of whisky with cobwebs on it; he had been saving it for a long time. It was unusual, then, for women to drink whisky with men, but everyone recognized that this was an occasion of which they had never seen the counterpart.

"Well, here's to the gone stock," Campbell said, his eyes on the liquor.

"And the better stock we aim to get," said Noah Bassett.

They tossed off the glasses without looking at each other. Then Jud Hyatt's fiddle began its last tune, and so weakened was the dying norther that the fiddle no longer had to rant and squall to make itself heard.

Soddy back of Silver Bow. . . .

They had heard Jud Hyatt play "Silver Bow Soddy" a hundred times, but they supposed now that they would never hear it again. It was a song in the old dance rhythms, half mocking, half roisterous, but at the same time very dear to the range with which they had struggled for so long.

And I suppose I'll never
See Bow Silver,
Silver back o' soddy.
Soddy back o' Silver,
Any time ever,
Any time ever.
Till I die.

That fiddle-ringing, boot-stamping refrain was going to come back to them all sometimes, growing dimmer and more vague, but never quite forgotten, through the years beyond.

The storm was a low uneasy moaning, almost the equivalent of a restful silence after the wild roar that had held on most of the night. They had half expected the blizzard to last two or three days, but the fact that it had died down after fifteen hours meant nothing. The prairie hay was a flattened tangle sheathed in glaze ice.

If a few bunches of the thaw-softened cattle had survived the terrible drop in temperature and the scour of the blizzard, they would still pay heavy toll. All signs suggested a long siege of bitter weather, and the Silver Bow owned no hay.

Jud Hyatt, the fire gone out of him, went into the lean-to room to get his sheepskin coat. He stood there alone, rubbing a clear place on the frosted pane, weary and more than half resigned at last. This was Jean's room. There were in it a light four-poster and a maple dresser that had come by oxen all the way from the Missouri. He was soaking up the feel of those things that she had lived close to, before it was too late. They would be gathering up the remainder of the stock, and moving it—some place. After that he would be riding on.

Beyond the ice-distorted face of the plain, the dawn was coming up out of the Cherokee country. It made a long line of silver-gray, with a drift of color delicate as wild rose blooms, on top. It was the time of day when Abe was generally getting ready to saddle, and saying always: "Well, it's another day."

Jean came in silently and stood beside him. He felt her fingers touch his hand, and he gripped them hard, but she did not flinch. They stood there close together, not looking at each other, or speaking, with their eyes on the far chill east, while slowly the light increased.

Lief Norgaard came clumping in behind him, and touched Hyatt on the shoulder. "You're wanted in here."

"All right." Hyatt shot a glance at Norgaard, and found that Lief's eyes were curiously baffled, filled with a flabbergasted wonderment. He followed Lief into the main room.

Luther Kendricks had a lot of papers on the table in front of him. He and Abe Campbell were in an argument, and old Abe seemed dazed. "I don't know what you mean," he kept mumbling.

"Anything's for sale," Kendricks growled. "You don't seem to understand me. You're to keep control. That's my system. That's always my system."

"But this"—fumbled Campbell—"this . . . there ain't anything to buy! Our notes. . . ."

"I've got a list of your notes," Kendricks told him. "Am I a child?"

"But what do you think you're buying, man? Not cows . . . there aren't any cows . . . not range, because the range is free."

"There's going to be cows," said Kendricks.

"You're buying. . . ."

"People!" roared Kendricks. "I buy people! I've never bought anything else but people. I keep telling you . . . that's my system. You think a bull-headed cowman can change my system now? I tell you I want Jud Hyatt . . . and you, Abe, and Lief, and the Bassetts. This range ain't hurt! All you need is money."

"All we need is . . . good God!"

"And I have it," said Kendricks. "Now I've got a kind of organization figured out. We'll keep the three brands separate as before. But. . . ."

Hyatt heard a choking catch in Jean's throat, and he followed her as she turned and fled. Behind the rough door of the lean-to, Jean collapsed, sobbing hysterically, into his arms.

He caught her up and laid her gently on the four-poster. Her fingers clung to his, so that he had to sit down on the edge. Softly he began to sing to her, whispering and low: " 'Better days . . . are humming in . . . the honeysuckle vine.' " He watched the young sunlight from the frosted pane come in and touch her hair with gold.

Jud said: "Soon as there's a let-up in the work, I'll be hauling timber . . . this ice will make fine sledding. You and I are going to have the prettiest house in the Silver Bow, in the spring."

Terlegaphy and the Bronc'

Fodder Williams, wandering bronc' peeler, had hung his rope on a close-coupled cayuse in the Triangle R breaking corral. He had snubbed the horse's head short to a post and put on the saddle blanket. The horse had stamped on his foot. Fodder, whose temper was short, had responded with an oath that smoked, and grabbed the quirt that dangled from his wrist, when. . . .

Whack! A hard old fist caught Fodder Williams back of the ear. It was a stinging blow, probably accompanied, in Fodder's head, by a great flash of light and the sound of distant thunder. The cowboy took three gigantic, hasty steps, such as any man takes when caught off his balance, and sprawled in the spring mud. He was up instantly and whirled with ready fists.

"Now, listen," said Whiskers Beck, backing away with his hands above his head. "Wait a minute! I didn't go fer to cause no bother! Now, listen!"

To be walloped behind the ear without notice is a surprise to most. But to whirl, with battle in your eye, to find a white-bearded attacker backing away with his hands up, and declaring that he didn't mean anything by it—that is astonishing. Fodder paused with fist drawn back for a shattering haymaker, and his mouth dropped open.

"Leave me explain," urged Whiskers. "Hold on now!"

Fodder recovered himself and started forward. "Why,

you . . . old. . . ."

Whiskers lowered his hands and ruefully braced himself to meet the attack. It didn't come. A restraining noose dropped over Fodder's shoulders and jerked his elbows against his sides.

"Now, here!" interposed Whack-Ear Bates, approaching hand over hand along the rope. "Mebbe you think you're havin' a scrap with Whiskers, but sech ain't the case! Anyways, not till I'm topped off. 'Smatter with you?"

Fodder Williams was a man extremely willing with his fists. But he was only a medium-size man, and Whack-Ear's lean two hundred pounds towered above him like a coyote over a prairie dog. Fodder considered a moment as he shook loose the relaxed rope, and his wrath cooled somewhat.

"This bush-faced pelican went to work an' pasted me with a rock!" he declared.

"I done no sech thing," protested Whiskers. "I jest kinda patted him with the flat o' my hand to 'tract his attention."

"Why, you . . . !" began Fodder again, showing signs of action.

At this point old Ben Rutherford, the Old Man, stepped into the conference. "Whup! Pull up!" he put in. "Mostly my boys takes care o' themselves . . . but Whiskers is only about a hundred years old, an' a likely lad, and I don't want him all busted in pieces. You leave him be!"

"I guess I'm able tuh . . . ," began Whiskers.

Fodder slammed his five-pound hat against the ground. "You standin' there an' tellin' me I got to let every damn' fool in the outfit knock me down all he wants to?"

"Leave me explain," said Whiskers. "Didn't mean to cause no bother. But that bronc' there's jest exactly the hoss I been lookin' fer, fer a sartin partic'lar use. It took more'n three years tuh make that hoss, an' I don't perpose to have him spoiled by bein' hit with no quirt. So when Fodder hauls off at him, I had to take action sudden."

"Lemme get this straight," said the Old Man, shoving his broad hat to the back of his head. "You wallops this feller?"

"Yep."

"To stop him hittin' the *hoss?*"

"Yep!"

Three mouths dropped open as the men stared at Whiskers. A blank expression erased all signs of intelligence from the Old Man's craggy face. He and Whack-Ear looked at each other, dumbfounded.

"Well," said Old Man Rutherford finally, "it's a plumb mystery to me. But, Williams, you'll have to leave Whiskers be, that's flat. Either you calls off this deal or you kin move out!"

Fodder computed hastily. He knew that, if he quit, the story would go out that he had been whipped and driven off by a man old enough to be his great-grandfather. Such a story would never do for his future reputation on the range. He stalled for time.

"Look at them chaps!" he demanded. He pointed to the dirt that smeared the silky unclipped goat hair adorning his bowed legs. "Jest look!"

"Leave me have that cayuse, an' I'll clean them chaps up fine," offered Whiskers.

"How 'bout the hat?" pursued Fodder, picking up the article from where he had thrown it himself.

"All right . . . hat, too," conceded Whiskers.

"Take it or leave it lie," said Old Man Rutherford.

"I'll call quits," Fodder decided.

Whiskers heaved a sigh of relief. "Come on, hoss. Le's

you an' me go somewheres where it's quiet."

The three stared after him without comprehension as he led the dancing cayuse away.

"How yuh comin' with the specially eddicated bronc', Whiskers?"

Four days had gone by since Whiskers had knocked Fodder sprawling, and Whack-Ear thought the subject should now be cool enough for mess-shack handling.

"Fair," Whiskers reported. "Kettled somethin' terr'ble yestidday. Didn't know but what I'd bit off more'n I should, me bein' stiffer than once. That part's finished, though. Won't do no more than crow-hop to get warm from now on, I figger."

"I wouldn't give two cents for a horse that bucked only jest the once," said Dixie Kane. "Not one cent, even. Gimme a horse with sperrit . . . that fights back plenty!"

"This 'n's different," said Whiskers through a mouthful of hot potatoes.

"Get a real sperrited horse," said Dixie Kane. "Then get on an' ride . . . that's my way."

Whiskers gestured with his fork, gulped, and unlimbered into speech. "So I notice," he replied. "An' you never made a top hoss, neither. Some o' you rannies think if you can climb on an' stay on the top side that you know the whole works. Nossir. Trouble with you, yer ridin' hasn't been backed up by no readin'."

"Readin'?" repeated Doughnut Wilson, startled into unaccustomed speech. "What the . . . ?"

Squirty Wallace snickered and choked.

Whiskers went on unperturbed. "Betcha yuh never even heard about terlegaphy," he declared.

"Sure I did," Dixie Kane contended hotly. "You sends

somethin' through a wire, an' it comes out the other end in the shape o' rattles an' clicks."

"This here I got hold of is a new kind," said Whiskers. "I got it out of a newspaper. You sends a message from one brain to another, without wires nor nothin', jest by concentratin' the human eye. Hosses catches on special easy, bein' they use it theirself all the time.

"Now this here little hoss, Ten Spot, he's jest the hoss for that. I'm goin' to fix him so I kin operate him by terlegaphy, not hollerin' at him nor nothin'. Trouble with most cayuses is they're hard in the head, peetrified yuh might say. Ten Spot's different. What I think goes from my right eye to his temper'ment, like a magnet, an' there takes effect. Ten Spot, he's the right kind . . . hard in the muscle, but not in the head."

"Kind o' soft in the bean, huh?" said Whack-Ear. "Well, there's others."

"Mebbe," said Whiskers, wiping his brush-like beard with his sleeve. "Wait a while, an' we'll see."

He got up and strolled out, fumbling for his makings. Just around the corner of the mess shack he brought them to light, and paused to light a cigarette. He could hear the voices within.

"He's goin' to work an' spoilin' a good fast horse," said Dixie Kane. "When a horse don't fight back right, why, somethin's wrong either in horse or handlin'."

"He makes me sick," said Fodder's voice. "If, now, jest f'r instance, somebody would take an' sling their hat down in front o' that bronc', jest as he was ridin' him out . . . I wonder now if what follered wouldn't set 'em both into righter ways o' thinkin'!"

"Yep," said Whack-Ear. "On'y, anybody won't, or hadn't better."

"Well, there's a whole hell of a lot of won'ts around this outfit," answered Fodder. "That's all I got to say!"

Whiskers walked to the bunkhouse and got his old six-shooter out of his bedroll, and, when Fodder came up, Whiskers was sitting on a bench outside, cleaning the gun with care.

"What's all that for?" Fodder asked casually.

Whiskers looked at him with a slow, baleful gaze.

"Well," he said, "if everythin' goes jest to suit me, I'm goin' to shoot a yalla praira dog someday." He got up, stuck the iron in its open holster, hooked the slit thong over the hammer, and strolled off toward the corrals.

Fodder stared after him. *Crazy-loco,* he told himself, *an li'ble to go hurtin' somebody, like as not. Somethin' oughter be done 'bout that.* He scratched his head. *Mebbe, too, I'm the one that oughter do it, come a chance!*

Whiskers began Ten Spot's education when the first green grass was showing at the edge of the melting snow. For four weeks Fodder Williams, Dixie Kane, and Charley Decatur worked in the breaking corral, peeling the raw bronc's that had been hazed in with the range stock. The winter riders, together with a half dozen 'punchers who had wintered in town and several new hands, amused themselves topping off the strings of saddle stock that were cut to them. And Whiskers worked chiefly on Ten Spot.

By the time that the wagons pulled out for the spring roundup, Whiskers was more confident than ever that Ten Spot was the makin's of probably the best—and certainly the most terlegaphic—cow horse in three remudas.

From time to time Whiskers would demonstrate to skeptics how terlegaphy worked in practice. He would walk out to the edge of the remuda, and pick a point possibly fifty yards from Ten Spot. Then, without saying a word, he would fold his arms and subject Ten Spot to a piercing glare. The ragging of the other 'punchers was somewhat diminished by the fact that Ten Spot actually came. Doughfoot Wilson, at least, was sufficiently impressed to try it himself, but, as nothing happened, he gave it up and returned to "talkin' down a rope."

Most, however, thought they perceived a connection between Whiskers's terlegaphy and Ten Spot's taste for fresh bread, and said so. Nevertheless the most unimpressed were willing to admit that Whiskers's tutelage was developing Ten Spot into a willing and brainy little cow horse.

Spring breezed past, and the early roundup was over. Riders rode out singly, or in little groups of twos and threes, to hunt out the scattered wild cattle that the roundup had missed, with a view to decorating calf hides with brands. These were often gone many weeks at a time, living off the country when their scant rations were exhausted. So the summer ran its course.

Then, as the first frosts began to turn the prairie wool the color of dusty leather, the cook once more yelled at his six-horse team, and the chuck wagon rolled. Charlie Decatur, the pilot, rode in the lead, and the bed wagon and the wood wagon swung in behind. Following these came the remuda—the herd of saddle stock—and sixteen or seventeen 'punchers rode where they pleased. The fall works were on.

Ten Spot was now rounding into a mighty neat little cow horse, one that showed an intelligent interest in his work. Whiskers was working harder than ever to make Ten Spot strictly terlegaphic, and seemed to be having some success.

The test of Whiskers's terlegaphy theory came in the fall roundup's third week.

* * * * *

Whiskers had in mind several fine points in the education of Ten Spot, which he conceived could be best taught out of sight and sound of the herd. He wanted to teach him, for instance, the uncommon knack of driving two or three steers in a constant direction without frequent correction by his rider. He wanted him to know the vagaries of a lone steer on the open plain, as differing from those of a steer near a herd, and other points leading to the consummation of his ideal.

"Whack-Ear," said Whiskers to the straw boss, "reckon if I'd ride back north'ard a ways I might pick up quite a little bunch of stray critters."

"Take a look," said Whack-Ear.

Whiskers Beck, therefore, tied three days' very scant rations and a couple of blankets to his saddle, and, without further ado, rode north.

He swung in a wide circle, so planning that, when his chuck gave out, he would be not more than nine hours easy ride from the main herd. Hunting was for some reason not so good as he had expected. On the morning of the fourth day he was not more than four hours' jog from the herd, driving only two hobbled steers. A little after midday he jumped at a third steer.

The animal, evidently a wise old-timer, had been lying low in a bunch of brush, and Ten Spot was almost upon the steer before it broke. The horse leaped in pursuit, overtaking the steer in easy bounds. Whiskers tossed his rope over the long horns and jerked it taut. Ten Spot was fast catching on to this part of the job. The buckskin pony swung round the hindquarters of the steer to the far side and raced ahead. The steer, his hind legs jerked from under him, crashed to the ground in a cloud of dust.

Ten Spot stopped and leaned on the rope. Whiskers was already off, running to the steer. Quickly the old 'puncher hog-tied one foreleg to the two hind hoofs. Then he calmly sat on the steer's carcass and rolled a cigarette.

"Real good, Ten Spot. Make a hoss yet, iffen you keep tryin'."

Leisurely he smoked the cigarette and rested, watching with pleasure the patience with which Ten Spot stood to the rope. Presently he tossed away the fag, loosed the lariat, coiled it, and hung it on the saddle. Next he tied the steer's off hind hoof to its near fore with a short piece of rope.

Whiskers remembered afterward that he had looked at that bit of rope with suspicion. It was pretty old, cut from a worn-out lariat. But. . . .

"Iffen it busts, we got more," said Whiskers.

Now he passed the steer's tail between its hind legs, took a firm grip with one hand, and with the other loosed the piggin' string.

Twelve hundred pounds of beef struggled to rise. Whiskers hung on the tail, pulling upward, and the steer stayed down. In a few moments the big black beast gave it up.

"Now, c'mere," said Whiskers to Ten Spot. Still dimly trying to please, Ten Spot came three steps closer.

"Little more," demanded Whiskers.

Ten Spot advanced one step.

"More yet!"

Ten Spot lowered his head and whuffed at the steer with an air of distrust, then advanced a very scant foot.

"Oh, all right," said Whiskers. "Guess the old man can make it from here."

Whiskers suddenly released the steer's tail and bolted for his saddle. He saw Ten Spot shuffle nervously, and knew the big black critter was surging to his feet. In that instant a dog hole caved under Whiskers's foot, and he plunged headlong, almost against his horse's cannon bone. Ten Spot shied in a sidelong leap that took him yards beyond Whiskers's reach. The old man heard the snap of the breaking hobble, and a furious *thud* of hoofs.

Instantly Whiskers snatched his iron from its open holster, cocked the pistol with the same motion that flicked the slit thong of the hammer, rolled over on his elbow, threw up the barrel—all in less than a second—and pulled the trigger.

A dull *click* responded, then a second, as he pulled again. Flying hoofs, red eyes, a tremendous sweep of horns were almost upon him. Whiskers rolled like a flash toward the charging beast. Horns and hoofs passed over.

The man twisted head and shoulders and, with elbow resting on the ground, pulled the trigger four times as the steer whirled and returned to the charge. Not one shot answered. A terrible sickening sensation gripped the old man's vitals, the sensation of a weaponless man facing imminent death.

As the hammer *clicked* harmlessly upon the last chamber, Whiskers threw out the cylinder and snapped the ejector. Six empty shells fell into the dust. His left hand shot to a chap pocket. Once more that great horned head flashed above him. He rolled toward the trampling hoofs. The fore hoofs passed over. One sharp, iron-hard hoof spurned his left knee with a vicious grind.

In a deep corner of the pocket Whiskers's fingers found a cartridge. With hand shaking a little with haste, he popped the cartridge into the chamber, snapped the cylinder into place. The steer was charging again. This time the gun spoke with a heavy *crash,* and the steer went down.

"Well, gosh-a'mighty," said Whiskers peevishly, "it's pretty damn' near time!"

He sat up and examined his numbed knee ill-humoredly. The pain was just beginning to course through it with the throbbing return of the blood. A warm trickle along his thigh told him that the knee was beginning to bleed. He decided to take off his weather-stiffened chap and see if a bandage would help. With his hands he gingerly bent the leg.

"Wowie! Hold on, cowboy!" he addressed himself. "We jest better let well enough be. Me, I'm goin' home!"

He tried to get to his feet. It was no use. It simply couldn't be done. Now, if ever, was the time to send a few urgent mental messages to his horse. He rested painfully on his elbow and concentrated mind and eye on Ten Spot.

Ten Spot had discreetly retired from the scene of action, and was now grazing a hundred yards away. Whiskers fixed him with a sincere glare, and sent him a mental telegram that fairly shot sparks. Nothing happened. Perhaps, after all, terlegaphy was unable to carry over so great distances. When several minutes of this brought no more favorable results, Whiskers tried other resources. He whistled sharply to attract the pony's attention. Ten Spot looked up and favored Whiskers with a long, deliberate stare. Then he returned to his grass.

"Hey, there!" shouted Whiskers. "You know what I mean! Come over here! Mind, now!"

No sign of intelligence from Ten Spot.

The old man began to swear. A thin stream of scorching invective trailed across the prairie to Ten Spot. The horse grazed steadily, unimpressed. Whiskers changed his tactics.

"Beans, Ten Spot!" he called persuasively. "Openin' up a nice, juicy can o' beans! Come an' get 'em! Don't you want beans?"

Ten Spot gave no sign that he had heard. Possibly he preferred tangible grass to imaginary canned goods. In any case he stayed where he was. Terlegaphy and the human voice alike failed to dent Ten Spot's brazen indifference. He had evidently discovered that he didn't have to obey.

When a horse won't come to you, it is necessary to go to the horse. Whiskers's injured knee was now paining him badly. His left foot was beginning to swell, and with great difficulty he worked off the loose boot with the toe of the other. Then, dragging the boot in one hand, he began to crawl toward the horse.

Slowly, painfully, he pulled himself across the level ground. The sock dragged off of the bootless foot; a little trickle of blood appeared on the ankle and began to dot his trail with little dark spots. Every inch of the way was torture, but inch by inch, foot by foot, he somehow covered the ground. From time to time Ten Spot moved forward in his grazing, undoing in a moment five minutes of agonizing toil.

Whiskers knew that the nearer he approached Ten Spot without attracting the animal's attention, the surer was his chance of success. He paused and rested ten yards from the mount, then forced himself to go on. Five yards. Ten Spot was headed the other way. Just a little farther, he told himself. Two yards more.

"C'mere, Ten Spot!" His voice sounded strange, a hoarse, raucous croak.

Ten Spot started, spun about, and gazed at the grotesque, sprawling figure of the man. Perhaps a faint scent of blood came to his nostrils. He whuffed, shook his head, and started away at a lope. One fore hoof stepped on the trailing reins, jerking down his head, and the horse somersaulted. Badly scared, the pony scrambled to his feet and went into a mad fit of bucking as he plunged away. Then he straightened out and ran.

Ten Spot was half a mile away when he began to graze again. Whiskers's face became gray and set as he stared at the distant horse. Without even an oath the old man gritted his teeth and started the long drag in pursuit. The pain in his leg was now almost unbearable, running in hot surges well up into his back. The blood still trickled slowly, draining his strength. It left little blackening dots in the dust of the plain. Once he collapsed face down, his laboring breath drawing little particles of sand between his dry lips, and, when he tried to spit it out, he could not.

Yet he went on and on, ever so slowly covering the ground, while the hours passed and the sun went down. Finally, somehow, three quarters of a mile from the carcass of the steer, he found himself once more one hundred yards from his horse. Whiskers regarded with dull eyes the animal that meant life, hope, the only chance he had to avoid a slow death on the plain.

The bleeding had stopped at last, but he was weak. He had not eaten since sun-up, and this, with the loss of blood, left him faint. His head pounded and swam, and gradually the prairie floor assumed a slow, hardly perceptible revolving motion that told him he had not much farther to go.

The sun was setting now behind the far Wind River Mountains, spreading over the softening sky a glory of wine purple and Aztec gold that Whiskers did not see. And with the sunset there came a far-off sound that brought the cold sweat to the old man's brow.

It began in a low, moaning thunder, the deep-lunged bass of a restless bull. It increased in volume till the great voice broke into bleating soprano bellows. No personality in the herd is so subject to malevolent whim as the bull. He can be as docile and timorous as any calf, or, sometimes, he can work himself up to prowl and stamp half the night, with enraged roars, over half a tin cupful of spilled blood. Not a fearsome sound, this bellowing, to a man in the saddle or by a fire, but an ominous thing to a crippled man alone on the plain, lying at the end of a dotted trail of blood. Slowly Whiskers twisted his head and looked back the way he had come. He could see the cattle, perhaps a dozen of them, a low black blur three quarters of a mile away. The bull he could not make out, but Whiskers knew that he was probably sniffing the blood of the fallen steer, and throwing dirt over his own back with pawing hoof.

Whiskers thrust a shaking hand into the pocket that had yielded the stray cartridge, in the desperate hope that another might be there. The pocket contained tobacco crumbs, lint—nothing more. Hastily the old man began searching the other pockets in his clothes.

"God . . . !" he whispered fervently. "Leave me have jest one. For God's sake be there. *Be* there."

One was. Shakily Whiskers put the lone remaining cartridge into his gun. Then, with clamped teeth and features contorted with pain, he began the traversing of that last hundred yards to Ten Spot. Slowly, very slowly, he made his way, pausing frequently to husband strength. It was like the nightmare torture of a fever dream. Nearer now sounded the deep, moaning voice of the bull. *Mwaaaw . . . mmmwaaaaaw!*—a malevolent, evil thing.

Twenty minutes passed. The clear night of evening was dimming into dusk. Whiskers looked back. He could make out the bull now, a great dark beast in advance of his little band of staring cattle. He could see him sniff and paw. Unquestionably he was following up that crooked, tortured trail. The man turned his eyes to Ten Spot, thirty yards away.

The horse had ceased to graze and was half turned,

staring back. Perhaps he was suspiciously regarding the huddled figure on the ground, perhaps looking at the approaching cattle beyond. On what the animal would do next depended Whiskers's chance for life.

The old man gauged the distance. Little use, the single cartridge, to kill the bull, if the other cattle followed in a trampling rush, or if Ten Spot once more cantered beyond his reach into the dusk. Whiskers made a brave decision. Drawing his revolver, he staked his life on a single flip of the cards.

He braced his elbows and aimed with both hands at the top of Ten Spot's neck. A graze shot could drop the horse, momentarily stunned. A fraction of an inch too high would miss; an equal strength margin too low would kill. Either error would mean the end.

His hands shook, and he dared not shoot. Three times he closed his eyes and lowered the gun to steady his trembling hands. On the fourth attempt he fired, and Ten Spot fell.

Scrambling, regardless now of pain, Whiskers clawed himself over the ground, any old way, desperately striving to reach the pony before he should rise, if, indeed, he were ever to rise again. He reached the fallen horse, dragged himself over Ten Spot's barrel, and clutched the horn. A long moment passed, the horse motionless beneath him, not seeming to breathe.

Mwaaaaw . . . mmmwaaaw! said the voice of the bull, very close now, so close that when he stood and pawed, Whiskers could hear his hoof tear at the earth. The old man rested. He was through, his last card played. It was already decided whether he had lost—or won.

Ten Spot stirred, then rolled over on to his knees, and shook his head. With a mighty effort Whiskers got his sound leg over the saddle. The pony heaved to his feet.

"It's me, Ten Spot!" Whiskers croaked. "It's me! Whoa an' easy, in the name o' God!"

Somehow Whiskers recovered the trailing reins, and held the pony to a jogging walk until he could fumblingly strap himself to the saddle by buckling front and rear coat straps through his belt. His released bedroll slid off, but he didn't care. He let the reins fall over the pommel and held on with both hands. With the battle over, his game old nerve gave out, and the tears ran into his beard.

Ten Spot skirted the little herd of cattle, and headed south for the remuda, far away.

"Seems like . . . we're goin' . . . the wrong way," said Whiskers through the mists of pain.

He vainly tried to turn Ten Spot with his sound leg. Ten Spot went on.

Dawn and a creeping grayness. Then two long streaks of burnt orange came into the buckwheat sky just above the eastern horizon, like long trailers of bright smoke.

At the main herd camp of the Triangle R, one of the motionless rolls of blanket emitted a preliminary whimper, growled, and disgorged a tousled and bleary-eyed cook, fully dressed. This abused-looking husky stumbled over to the next roll of blanket and nudged it with his boot.

"Huh," he said to it in a tone of command. " 'Snother day."

A puff-eyed 'puncher struggled to a sitting position and shook the next man.

With sleepy but effective movements the cook was starting his fire. The two wakened 'punchers pulled on their boots, picked up rope and rig, and stumbled off toward the remuda, preparing to relieve the two motionless statues riding night herd a quarter of a mile away. An encouraging smell of bitter black coffee began to drift over the camp; a great mass of potatoes began to sizzle; the fire cracked and smoked. Blanket rolls stirred and subsided, the men inside groping for a last brief catnap before the ordeal of getting into action.

Whack-Ear, deep within his blankets, woke slowly, and painfully considered the necessity of rolling out. Some feeble fumbling cleared his head of the blankets; he yawned—and then listened. The soft *plunk* of walking hoofs sounded close, very close. In another moment a hoof moved into his line of vision and stopped. Whack-Ear twisted his neck, and with sleepy stupidity made his eye trace up a foreleg to the horse at the end of it. Suddenly Whack-Ear burst out of his blankets with a great yell.

"For God's sake, look here!"

All around him heads thrust sleepily out of blanket rolls. They stared for a fraction of a moment, then their owners, like Whack-Ear, turned out with sudden alacrity. A cluster of serious-faced 'punchers quickly formed about the invading horse.

In the middle sat Whiskers, slumped over the pommel, gripping the horn with white, stiff hands. One leg, crooked and unnatural, stuck out stiffly away from the stirrup. He looked at them uncomprehendingly, with haggard, staring eyes that seemed set in black pits.

Whack-Ear and Squirty Wallace were fumbling at the straps that tied the old 'puncher to the saddle. Whiskers opened his mouth and tried to speak, but only a rasping noise came forth. Then, with a great effort, he wrenched out a question.

"Which o' you boys," he croaked, "took the cartridges . . . out o' . . . my iron?"

No one answered.

Whiskers slowly moved his haggard blank eyes over the group of 'punchers. "I know!" he rasped, fixing his gaze upon Fodder Williams. "That's the one!" He let go the horn, and stretched a stiff, shaking claw in Fodder's direction. "You . . . yalla . . . coyote . . . I'll fix . . . your dirty works."

Whiskers gripped the pommel and gamely tried to swing himself out of the saddle. Then suddenly he collapsed into Whack-Ear's arms.

"If I was you, Fodder," said Whack-Ear presently, "I b'lieve I'd take my horse an' ride."

Fodder, having considered the matter from all angles, took his horse and rode.

"Terlegaphy?" said Whiskers a long time after to a not-too-cautious questioner. "Terlegaphy? 'S'all right, son, works real slick an' inflooential . . . sometimes. But when it ain't workin' . . . well, you best do like me. Send that or'nary, obstinate, wooden-headed crocodile some other sort o' message . . . one that'll be real pressin'!"

Gunfight at Burnt Corral

When a story is being told about a man, he himself is the last one to hear it. So it was a long time before I found out what was being told about the part I played in the gunfight up at Burnt Corral. But now I tell you that I was the last one who should have got any name out of that fight. It was Jim Flood who made that fight, Jim Flood as good as alone, one man against four, and I was no good.

That thing came at the end of the most haywire two weeks of my life, and those two weeks came at the end of the worst year I ever had, and I was feeling mighty sunk. I still think the Flying M that I rode for that year was in the right. The big Salinas crowd, made up of four or five big brand outfits, was warring it out with three or four little outfits like the Flying M, such as could only have one or two riders, and the idea was to rough our little outfits and worry us always, until we were rubbed out of the range.

It was the same old story of war over grass and water, with the same old finish—the little ones being beaten and crushed out by the big ones. But though the end was written in the beginning, it seems an end to such a thing can't come without three or four good boys being leveled off and spaded under the plain. Of course, that had happened here.

I was only a hired hand for the Flying M, but I had ridden mighty hard and steady for that outfit, and I swear to you I had seldom given an inch to the riders of the Salinas crowd. The same was true of Bud Cary, my side rider, the Flying M's only other cowboy. The Salinas crowd killed Bud Cary at Wolf Head Water Hole. Later they tried to get me at Paintrock Gap, but there I had the luck to kill the man who had killed Bud, and I got away.

Just about then the Flying M owners had enough, and they quit cold. They quit the valley and they quit cattle and they quit me. It seems the big outfits always have the law with them, and the Flying M owners had found it needful to clear themselves by denying all knowledge of shooting orders, and blaming me.

So there I was, outlaw, without hope of justice, and no loyalty left to anything—worn out and broke, and hunting a hole to crawl into, which came mighty hard.

Late in the day of August 31st, I was working my horse up through the bouldery bed of the Little Stormy, which was almost dry from the fading out of the snows above. That day I had come all the way from the floor of the desert up into the timber belt, where the Dragoon Mountains stand, gaunt and straight, pushing their granite into the sky.

I was still trying to break loose and head south for the Mexican border, but they were checking the country so close there was small chance of making it through, unless I could get rested, and somehow get hold of fresh horses. For I had ridden the same horse a week, and he was all but finished.

So I had spent the last of his strength making it into this high, lost crack in the Dragoons, where I knew there was an abandoned miner's cabin, and usually a grub cache. And here I meant to lay over a little while, until I could decide what I'd better do.

A little before sundown, I rode into the meadow that was

well known to the boys as the Burnt Corral. I can tell you it looked good to me, cupped in among those almighty tall Dragoons, still and quiet, with plenty of water, and fetlock-deep grass that was actually green, from the *ciénaga* seep. On the far side was the little cabin, made of logs instead of adobe like the outfits down below, and I was hoping I would find some beans and bacon here, as well as rest for a saddle-weary man.

Then, as I came within the last hundred yards, I pulled up and sat listening. I don't know what warned me. The quiet was unbroken, but somehow I knew that something was wrong, and that this was a place I shouldn't have come to. I must have sat there in the saddle for five minutes before I pushed my pony up near the cabin, moving slowly.

Then suddenly there was a girl standing in the cabin doorway, looking at me. She had stepped there without any sound, just as if she had appeared out of nothing. She had a carbine slung in the crook of her arm.

I suppose I never saw a more unwelcome sight. That girl standing there meant finish for me. It didn't even matter whether she was alone or not. I didn't need the cabin any more than a coyote does, and I could probably talk her out of the bacon and beans. But, above all, I needed grass and water for my pony, and there wasn't the equal of the Burnt Corral for that in another day's ride. And I knew that as soon as I had pulled out, she would hightail downcountry and give the alarm, and the posses would be closing in, and just about all the chance that was left would be gone.

Yet, even then, bad as she made things look for me, I realized that she made a mighty pretty picture standing there in the long clear twilight. She was a slim, straight girl, with a thin lively face. Her short tawny hair was rumpled up all wild and loose, and she had straight eyes that never flickered.

"You're Kit Palmer," I said at last.

"And you're Bill Saunders," she said, "wanted for the killing at Paintrock Gap."

I don't think I had ever spoken to her before, but each of us knew who the other was, all right. Her father was Sundown Palmer, one of the Salinas crowd that had busted the Flying M, and was now after my scalp. I don't know why a tough old character is called a sundowner in some parts of the West, but that is how Sundown got his name. And this girl, pretty as she was, was well able to take care of herself on her own account. Deer hunting was her game, and she thought nothing of going off on a week's hunt, alone in the hills.

"I wasn't exactly expecting you," Kit Palmer said.

"Naturally," I said. "I didn't know you'd took over this stand, or I wouldn't be here."

"This is anybody's shack that wants to use it, I guess."

"And first come has water rights," I answered. "So me, I'll be moving on."

"I don't know as you will," Kit Palmer said. "There's a reward up for you, my gun-throwing friend."

I said: "There isn't anything you can do to stop me, I guess."

"I can drop you out of the saddle as easy as I'd drop a bird," she said, letting the carbine swing loose and easy on her arm.

I sat there in the saddle and studied her, and I still thought that she made a mighty pretty picture, standing there in her cowboy clothes, on her slim long legs. She was good-looking enough in her sort of way, but I was tired and I lost my temper.

"I'm going to turn my horse and be out of here," I told her. "It would be like a Palmer to shoot a rider in the back. But you're not going to do it, because you lack what it takes. You're going to watch me ride out of here without even raising your gun, and, even if you do raise it, you won't be able to get the trigger pulled."

"No?" she said.

"No. I can even tell you what you'll do next. You'll saddle up and go downcountry and run yipping to the Salinas coyote pack, and tell 'em where I'm to be found. I know your kind and your breed. I know you right down to the ground."

Even in the dark I could see how white she had turned under her tan. I grinned, feeling very bitter. Then I turned my worn-out horse, and I walked him toward the upcountry trail.

A black silence shut down as I turned my back on Kit Palmer. All I could hear was the *swish* of my pony's slow hoofs, as he stumbled in the grass. I didn't know whether Sundown Palmer's daughter raised her gun on me or not, and I didn't much care. I rode across the meadow toward the dry trail above.

Then I heard a pony behind me, and I knew that Kit Palmer was coming after me. Wearily I figured that she had decided to make one more bluff to hold me for the posse. I faced my horse around and let her come up.

She had jumped on her pony bareback, and her hair was floating in the wind as she came tearing up. But when she had brought her pony to a stop, she didn't seem to know what to say.

"Well," I said, "what is it now?"

"You're wrong about the Palmers," she said in a queer voice. "No Palmer ever shot anybody in the back."

"They shot Bud Cary in the back at the Wolf Head," I reminded her.

"That was Jap Connolly did that," she said. "I don't hold it against you that you downed Connolly when they jumped you at Paintrock Gap."

This was a surprise, and I began trying to figure what kind of a shenanigan she was working on now.

"I don't throw guns around at anybody from either behind or in front," she went on, still talking kind of queer. "And another thing I don't do is run yipping to turn a posse onto an all-in man on a half-dead horse. I don't recognize you, and I didn't see you here. You're welcome to the cabin and the feed."

I sat and stared at her, and finally I began to believe she meant what she said. "I'm ashamed of the way I spoke to you," I said.

"Forget it. Cut loose your pony and we'll cook up a few venison steaks."

I would have been a fool not to take her up on that. We rode back to the little cabin. But before swinging down, I sat quietly on my horse in front of the door, listening. The girl dropped off her pony. Then, seeing what I was doing, she stood still and listened, too.

"There's another horse coming up the Little Stormy," she said, after a minute.

I drew a deep breath and I felt weak, for she was right.

Kit Palmer said: "You'd better swing your horse around the cabin and fix to pull out through the trees, if you need to. And maybe you'd better shift your saddle onto my horse."

God knows I didn't feel like fighting, but I didn't want to run out with the girl's horse, either. As I stalled and argued, the rider from downcountry came into view, and it was too late.

The clear sunset light was still hanging on, and even at the quarter mile I recognized the bald-faced roan horse and knew who the rider was.

The girl knew as quick as I did. "It's Jim Flood!" she said, and I partly knew why she spoke so sharp. "Is he on the gun for you?"

"Not that I know of."

Still, in the uncertain way I was living, I figured it would be best to make sure, so I went out to meet him, riding at a walk. We met out in the meadow well out from the cabin, and both reined up and sat sizing each other up. I knew his name, and I supposed he knew mine, but I'd never talked to him before.

Jim Flood had been holding down the same job with the little Lazy J that I had had with the Flying M, except that I was supposed to be just a cowboy while Flood was supposed by everybody to be there because he was a gunfighter who had made his name out-country on warrior jobs. Having heard so often how bad he was with a gun, I was kind of surprised at the way he looked up close, for he didn't look like a tough one at all, but like a happy-go-lucky kid.

"What the hell are you doing here?" he said unfriendly.

There never had been any love lost between the Flying M and the Lazy J, even though we were on the same side of the war. But while my owners had turned against me, his boss had been run out of the country altogether, so there wasn't any great reason for enmity between us. Still, the way he had come at me, there wasn't anything I could do or say.

"I don't guess I ever learned to hear that brand of question, Flood," I told him.

He was looking past me, very steady, and now it suddenly came to me why he had come at me on the prod. Everybody knew that Jim Flood was dead gone on Kit Palmer, and though it drove her father crazy, Sundown Palmer hadn't been able to keep him from seeing her sometimes. Now that Flood saw that she was here, I figured it probably steamed him up because I was here with her. When a man is crazy about a girl, he isn't always reasonable.

"You got no business even being in the same country with her," he said now.

"I guess," I answered, "that's for her to say, and not you."

"Maybe," he said. "I'm still enough people to decide some things like that."

"Meaning?"

"You're moving on."

"No," I said. "I'm not moving on, nor taking orders from you in any shape or way."

His face changed. I saw his eyes flicker to my gun, and his own hands were light and ready together in front of him on his reins.

Kit Palmer had been riding out toward us, and now she was with us before we knew it. "Jim," she said in a despairing voice, "what's the matter with you now?"

Jim Flood looked at her steady. "Kit," he said, "go back. I have to talk to this man, and you have to go back."

He meant it to be an order, but it didn't sound convincing. He must have known that Kit Palmer wouldn't move.

"Jim, if you fight again . . . here and now . . . I'll never speak to you again."

I don't think he believed her.

After a minute or two he said: "All right, Kit."

"I got some shot meat here," Kit Palmer said. "We'd better all have something to eat now, I should think. I'm going to go back and cook." She turned and rode toward the cabin.

Jim Flood and I looked at each other a minute, and then, a little sheepishly maybe, we followed her pony.

"This thing isn't over," Flood said. "We've got to have it out, later on."

"That's all right with me."

We rode up to the cabin, and Flood threw down his saddlebags and his blanket roll. Then I began getting wood in, and one thing and another like that, while Kit Palmer set in to cook some meat. Flood rode off to the edge of the meadow and put his horse up a climb. I knew that he was taking a look out in the last light where he could see the back trail down Little Stormy.

It was dark, and the meat was ready by the time he got back. Kit and I had dug up a couple of old lamps, and they were lighting the cabin in a smoky way. Jim Flood came and stood in the doorway, his eyes on Kit Palmer.

"Kit," he said, "I got to tell you something."

"I'm not asking any questions," Kit Palmer told him.

"This ropes you in as well as me," Flood said. "I guess it ropes all three of us."

Kit looked at him. "Jim, you've been in a fight?"

"Kit, I swear I could've downed them all," Flood said. "I had to gun two of them to get clear. One I took through the arm because it was him or me, and one I brought off his horse with a bullet in his leg, because his horse was better than what I had. It was the least I could do, if I was going to get clear."

Kit said: "Thank you, Jim. But I don't think we have got to talk about it now."

"That's just the trouble. We do have to talk about it. I thought I gave them the slip before I made my break up the Little Stormy. I've just found out that I didn't give them the slip. Four deputies from Salinas are riding up the Little Stormy. Right now they're within a mile. They're wanting Bill Saunders, here . . . and they're wanting me."

There was a long moment of silence, then Kit said: "You'll have to get out, Jim. Both of you have to get out!"

Jim Flood shook his head. "This is the first time I ever ran for it in my life. I couldn't have done it except for you . . . and, even for you, I can't keep on."

"But if you let them take you back. . . ." There was fear in Kit Palmer's face. She knew as well as we did what kind of trial either one of us would get if they took us back.

"I can't let them take me back."

"But if you stand and fight. . . ."

"Kit, this time I can't fight, either. One of the deputies is your father."

There was silence again while they looked at each other.

Kit Palmer cried out: "Jim, you can't fight him!"

"Of course, I can't fight him."

"But if you won't ride?"

"I've run from them once. That was once too much. If I do it again I'll never be able to live with myself. I'll run no more."

Suddenly Kit Palmer moved quickly toward the door.

Jim caught her with: "Where you going?"

"I'm going out to meet them and turn them back."

Flood smiled and shook his head. "They know now by the sign that whoever is up here has not been here alone. Both Saunders's horse and mine show tracks in the sand pockets of the Little Stormy. You can't do it, Kit."

Real terror came into Kit's face. "In heaven's name,

what are you going to do?"

"I'll try to bluff," Flood said. "They're scared of me . . . all except your father."

"But if they call your bluff?"

"I promise you this," Flood said. "Whatever breaks, I'll never raise a gun against him. Now you have to be moving out of here, Kit."

"Jim, I can't! If anyone can stop my father. . . ."

"It'll work just opposite, Kit. If he finds you here, he'll think you came here to meet me. That sounds like something I oughtn't to say, but you know it's true. He'll go broncho-wild if he thinks that. And you know what'll happen then."

All the life seemed to go out of Kit Palmer's face, and I saw her lips quiver, but then she seemed relaxed, resigned to whatever was ahead as she said at last: "All right, Jim. I'll go."

"Your pony's on picket?" he asked.

Kit Palmer nodded and walked to the door, slow. There she turned and looked at me. Until then, it seemed that they had both forgotten I was there. "And you," she said, "what will you do?"

"I'm staying."

Kit looked at Jim, and they held each other's eyes for a long minute. "Good luck to you," she said at last. Then she turned her eyes to me. "To you both," she added.

Then she was gone into the dark. Flood and I stood, neither of us moving until we heard her horse move off down the meadow on the upcountry side.

Flood moved across the room and blew out one of the lamps. He picked up a piece of meat and began to tear it with his teeth, looking at me as he ate. I picked up a piece of meat and bit into it, too. When I had wolfed it down, I rolled a cigarette and offered Flood the makings.

He wouldn't take them. "I'm not forgetting I still have a bone to pick with you when this thing is done."

I shrugged and let it go, and then we both stood listening sharply, for down at the lower end of the meadow a pony whinnied, and one of our own horses answered it from nearby.

"There they come," Flood said.

"You going to stay here, in the light?"

"Hell, yes. You still have time to take to the timber if you want."

I spit through my teeth to let him know what I thought of that crack, and after that we both shut up. Then for a long time there didn't seem to be anything to do but wait—the hardest thing that any man can possibly do in a case like that. I was wondering what Flood would try, and what I would try, when the posse came.

As I thought that over, I suddenly knew that I, too, could not throw a gun down on the father of this girl I had never talked to before tonight. There we were in the most cock-eyed situation I've ever seen—two of us who didn't dare be taken, yet seemingly were unable to run for it, either, while closing in on us in the meadow were three men and Sundown Palmer, the hard and unyielding old cattleman who we couldn't stand off nor fight nor kill.

We waited so long without hearing any more of the enemy horses that presently I knew what was happening out there and a cold snaky feeling went down my spine. They had left their horses tied at the lower end and had come on slow, spreading a little, maybe, to cover the door and all sides, if we should still try to make a break to get away.

After I had thought about that for a while I got so I

could feel them out there in the dark. I don't suppose we waited fifteen minutes while this went on, but it seemed like an hour. All that time Jim Flood sat with his knees crossed and the smoky lamp just over his shoulder on a little shelf. He was whistling softly through his teeth.

I was leaning against the wall to the side where the door was, so those just circling us outside couldn't see us, but I knew they must be able to see Jim Flood, and I wondered why he didn't worry for fear somebody would take a shot at him out of the dark. I thought the wait was never going to be over, but when it was over at last, it ended so suddenly that I was taken by surprise. I had imagined that I heard them all around us, moving in the dark, but it must have been imagination only, because, when Sundown Palmer stepped into the doorway, he got there silently, while I still didn't know anyone was within fifty yards.

"Reach," he said, his voice low but hard and sharp. His gun was in his hand, and his eyes were on Jim Flood.

Flood never stopped that gentle whistling through his teeth. His eyes had been on the floor, and now they drifted slowly up the long length of Sundown Palmer, until at last he looked Palmer in the eye. His hands were locked over one knee, easy and comfortable, and he didn't reach.

"Hello, Sundown," he said.

"Jim," said Sundown Palmer, very grim, "you're under arrest."

Jim Flood's eyes dropped to Sundown's gun, which was centered on the third button of Jim's shirt, and for a while Jim seemed to study that gun. Then his eyes turned to me, very noncommittal. Sundown wheeled quickly, to where he could more or less keep an eye on both of us at once, though his gun stayed on Jim. Until that moment I'm sure Palmer had not realized I was in the room.

Then he spoke to somebody outside. "Monk," he said, "step here."

After a moment or two, Monk Connolly stepped in and stood beside Palmer, and his gun was in his hand, too.

"We've got the two of them, instead of one," Sundown said.

Monk Connolly looked at me, and I saw his little eyes go red, redder than they were before, for this was a brother of Jap Connolly that I had shot it out with on the run when they jumped me at Paintrock Gap. I'll say this for Monk—he knew his business. Never minding anybody else, he kept his smoke-iron leveled on my belt buckle from then on. I thought there was a quiver in the muzzle of his gun, as if his trigger finger was itching to pull and square accounts for his brother Jap.

"You boys might just as well come," Sundown said slowly. "I don't know how you come to let me take the drop on you like you done, but there it is. I want you to reach high, and stay reached, while Monk takes off your guns."

"Sundown," Jim Flood said, "this war is over, and you've won. There isn't anything more left of the Lazy J. I can't let you take me in, and you know it. I tell you, I don't want to fight. You go your way, and I'll go mine. It looks to me like there's been enough blood spilled over this thing already."

Sundown Palmer's face didn't change from its hard set. "I'm not here working for my brand. I'm working for the law. I come out to get you and take you back, and I'm going to take you back. It's either up to you to reach and make no trouble or . . . make your play."

"It's your play, I think," Jim said.

"Have it your own way." Sundown sang out into the dark again: "Jack! Buck! Come on."

After a minute the two boys he had called came into the cabin. Jack Healy was one of those hangers-on around county offices that are always trying to wangle some favoritism job rather than go to work. The man they called Buck was a strong-shouldered guy with a big empty face.

"We can't take any chances with these babies," Sundown told these two. "Keep them both covered all the time. You go and take their guns off them . . . first Flood's gun, then Saunders's."

Jack Healy and the man called Buck moved toward Jim Flood, edging around behind Monk Connolly so that Monk could keep his gun on me all the time.

Then Flood's voice raised up, sharp. "Wait, Sundown! Let's talk. . . ."

"To hell with you! Go in on him, boys!"

Those were the last words spoken as the so-called Burnt Corral gunfight broke.

My eyes were on Jim Flood, and I saw him jump, as if dynamite had lifted him, from the pack box where he sat. His whole body shot up and to the side, and his left arm smashed that little lamp shelf, and the lamp went out of the world as if it had exploded. I must have jumped, too, at his first move, away from the wall, and dropped to my knees, for suddenly, without thinking about it, I was in the middle of the floor, and my gun was in my hand. Then hell broke loose in the dark of that God-forsaken cabin.

First there were two smashing reports, almost together, and those must have been the guns of Sundown and Monk Connolly. An instant before, they had been dead centered on Flood and me, and it's God's own wonder that they didn't get us both, but they did not. Then it seemed as if everybody must have been shooting; there were gun flashes everywhere.

I knew that Monk Connolly was lined up with the jamb of the door, and I lifted my gun and fired four times at where I thought he was. In the blasting of the guns, within those close walls, it was like being beat around the head with twenty clubs.

Then suddenly, just as suddenly as it had begun, that whole hell of gun noise stopped. There was dead silence in that black dark.

That silence seemed to hang on for minutes while I waited, trying to hold my breath and thinking I hadn't better move. Then, after a long time, somewhere outside I heard a horse take off on a run, downmeadow. We found out later that that was Jack Healy, the hanger-on from the county office. He had got part of a finger shot off, and he had lost his gun and his head.

Still I waited there in the dark. Then at last Jim Flood spoke. "Bill," he said, "are you there?"

"Yeah, I'm here."

"Are you hit? Can you strike a light?"

I was about to answer him when, somewhere in that room, someone moved—in a different place from where Jim's voice had come. Although I was taking what I thought was an awful chance, I fumbled for a match and struck it on the heel of my boot. If I live a hundred years, I'll never forget that instant when the light flared—first a daze in my eyes from the sudden flash, and then. . . .

The strange thing about anything like that is that everything comes out cock-eyed and irregular, nobody where you thought they were, or where there's any sense in their being. Jim Flood stood flat against the wall, in almost the exactly the place where the lamp had stood on the little shelf, except that now both the lamp and the shelf were gone. The man called Buck was down on his face close to the wall, in about the place I had been standing before the fight began.

Only Monk Connolly was where you might think he would be, and he was down in a heap just where he had stood, with one leg twisted under him so queer that even in the first glance I knew he was dead. I saw all that instantly, in a split second. It was Sundown Palmer who was the main figure in that room.

Sundown was in the strangest position of all. He was on one knee, his gun up and ready in his right hand, but somehow he had got turned around, so that he no longer faced Jim Flood but was facing the door. Almost in the instant that the match flared, he whirled as if he got his bearings instantly with the light, and his gun swung on Flood.

I should have fired on Sundown then, if only to try to break his arm, for I still had one cartridge left. Instead, I threw my gun at him from a distance of about ten feet, and it caught him under the ear just as he fired. The match went out as I threw the gun, and I fumbled after another one and lighted it.

Jim Flood still stood against the wall where he had stood before, but there wasn't any gun in his hand. Sundown was crumpled up, breathing very hard, in the middle of the floor.

Now I found the other lamp that had not been lighted when the posse came up. And I lighted it, clean forgetting that Jack Healy was unaccounted for and might be laying outside to put a gun in from the dark. It was only afterward we found he was gone.

When I turned around again, Jim Flood was pulling his brush jacket on, slow and deliberate. He looked white.

I began to choke up on what had really happened there. Monk Connolly was dead, sure enough, shot three times; but when I looked in the jamb of the door, I found my own four bullets planted high and loose—they hadn't hit anything or done any good. Then I saw the man called Buck open one eye, and I took his gun away. Nothing was the matter with him except he was shot through the thigh. That bullet was Jim Flood's, too. Now I did what I should have done in the first place, which was to disarm Sundown Palmer, for he was beginning to come to.

"We've done it now," I said to Flood. "Once we might have got by with a jury trial, but now . . . it's the wild bunch for us both, from here out."

"Yes," he said.

It seems crazy that I said what I did then, but it seemed the one thing I could say, at the time. "You still figure to pick a bone with me?" I asked.

"Yes," he said again.

"Then let's get it over with."

"I'm ready."

"Then go ahead and draw."

"Draw yourself," he said, looking me in the eye. "I'll be there, all right. Pull, if you're not too yellow!"

I thought I was against the tie-in of my life, and my hand dropped to my gun, and I drew . . . but I didn't fire.

Flood still stood motionless. His hand was still in his pocket. "You're yellow," he said. "Why don't you shoot?" He was standing with his back against the wall, the pack box between his knees, and I saw him slide gradually down, and then his head slumped forward. He toppled, and, if I hadn't caught him by the shoulders, he would have fallen off the box.

I hauled his brush jacket off. His right sleeve was soaking wet, for he had been shot through that arm. To save his life, he couldn't have made a draw, or even laid a finger on his gun. Even to get that hand to his pocket, he must have used his other hand. Yet Flood had dared me to draw, taunted me to draw, and then taunted me to fire!

I stopped the bleeding with strips of his own shirt, and then I tied up Buck's leg wound. Finally I got Sundown Palmer started off down the trail, with Buck whimpering with his wound, and Monk tied crosswise of his saddle. Only first I picked out their two best horses for Jim and me, and gave them ours.

I saw them off to the head of the trail—Sundown very black and grim as he led Monk's horse. He never looked at me or spoke. Then I went back to the cabin, knowing that we wouldn't have long to get on the move.

Kit Palmer was there when I got back. I guess she was dissatisfied with the way I had tied up Flood's arm, for she was re-bandaging it all, fresh and clean. Flood seemed to have explained to her what had happened, for they weren't talking, and she seemed to know all about it.

I stood and watched her work. Somber and broken as that night was, it seemed to me that I had never seen anything as sweet and as lovely as that girl, and it was strange to see her here in this place that still reeked of gunsmoke and battle. I can see yet the gentle, quick movement of her hands. The tears were running down her face all the time she worked, and somehow I blamed myself and Jim Flood, both, that this girl should ever have to be made to cry.

As she finished, he tried to kiss her, and she wouldn't let him. She just said: "Not now . . . not now."

Suddenly as I looked at her, it seemed to me the night air was fresh and clean, and I filled my lungs with it. All at once I found that I was feeling like a new man. The ugly feel of death and destruction went out of the night, and with it fear went out of me. I wasn't tired, and I wasn't discouraged.

I had no future, and a defeated past, and I was hopelessly outlawed, with no friend anywhere, no more than Flood. But I knew that someday all accounts would be squared, and that the Salinas crowd with all its greed and spite and hate would be showed up and broken, and those of us who had opposed them would be in the saddle again.

I knew that I would come back, and that someday I would win this girl. There wasn't a reason in the world to think all that, or to feel that way, but I somehow *knew*.

"We're on our way for a little while," I told Kit, when Jim Flood and I took to the saddle. For Jim had given in by then, and saw that his only chance was to ride for it, until his arm should heal. "We may be gone from here some little time, but in the end we'll be back."

"I hope so," Kit said.

I turned in the saddle and waved to her as we made the turn of the uptrail. She was still standing, looking after us, and she waved back. But Jim rode facing straight ahead, very pale. I don't think he believed we'd ever be back.

Along about dawn, high in the granites, I noticed Flood was looking at me very peculiar. I realized then that I had been singing—singing, by God!

"You feel good, don't you?"

"Yes," I said.

"You think you're coming back, and that this Salinas bunch can be beat?"

"Yes," I said again.

"You're gone on Kit," he accused me.

And I answered yes to that, too.

"You realize Kit's my girl? Yet you think you can take a girl from me?"

"Maybe I can."

Seemed like he didn't know what to think of that. "I'm

the better gunfighter," he told me, as if he was sizing me up all over again. "I'm a better cowboy, a better man with a bronc'."

"Yes," I said.

"Yet you think you can get my girl!" he said, as if he couldn't believe it.

"Jim, that's just what I'm going to do."

It seemed strange to be saying that, me an outlawed 'puncher without a dime or a hope, riding off a range because I was hunted off—and with small chance of even getting clear. But there in that dawn, dog-dirty, unshaven, and weary, I knew that what I told him was true.

"Maybe you and me better ride together a while, until things clear up," Jim said at last.

"OK, boy."

In the first daylight we topped One-eye Pass, and began dropping down into the badlands of the Walloon. Below us the hot shimmer of early sun on red rock was talking about bad days ahead, but in my eyes was a picture of a slim, straight girl with windblown hair, and I knew I was coming back.

A Horse for Sale

Old Man Coffee's three callers did not arrive together. Sheriff Pete Crabtree, with Mart Mosely trailing along behind him, came up the main trail while Bat Girard, starting from McTarnahan considerably later, took the rough cutoff and by smoky riding was able to arrive a few minutes ahead of the others.

Girard wasted no time in bursting into words. "Look here, Coffee . . . look here! That crooked bunch from downcountry have framed you up. They're going to make you look like a horse thief!"

"I don't deny," said Old Man Coffee amiably, "a slight facial resemblance to the lower classes. Howsoever . . . I misdoubt if they can prove it."

"They don't have to prove it," fumed Bat Girard. "You know what they want. They're dead set on sending Billy Johnson up for horse stealing, and you're his only witness! They're fixing to discredit you in front of the jury. And I just now found out what they've done. They've planted evidence on you! They've tooken a horse with Mosely's Feed Box brand on it, and they've tooken a knife and doctored it over into your Rocking Chair brand."

"Who done the doctoring?"

"I don't know for certain. Mart Mosely himself, most like . . . he sure must have had experience at it before he was run out of the Panhandle. This horse had one of these light-run brands that just shows as a ruffle in the hair. By curling the hair with your knife, you can add onto a brand like that so's you can't hardly tell it."

"I can show up a curled brand in two minutes," said Old Man Coffee contemptuously.

"How does that help you? That's just what *they* aim to do! And they've planted this horse not two miles from here. You know that old corral up Split Cañon? They've hid it there."

"There wasn't no horse there yesterday," said Coffee.

"They hid it last night!"

"What kind of looking horse did they use, I wonder?"

"It's that old sorrel Mosely generally rides to town on."

"Oho," said Coffee. "So that's the one. You *sure* of it?"

"Yes, dead sure, but. . . ."

"Then I've got him!" Coffee exulted. "By God, Johnson goes free!"

"But how the devil . . . ?"

His voice was drowned by the hammer of hoofs as Sheriff Crabtree came up. He dismounted and approached Old Man Coffee.

"There ain't anything personal in this," Crabtree apologized. "A couple of the boys rode in this morning with a crazy fool story, and certain parties have made a howl. So I've just rode up here to satisfy 'em more than anything else."

"That's nice of you," said Coffee.

"It seems a couple fellers rode through Split Cañon yesterday," Pete Crabtree went on, "and they seen one of Mart Mosely's horses hid in that old corral there. They claim they seen your brand on it."

"In short," said Coffee, "it's supposed to look like I stole a horse." He gazed pointedly at Crabtree's companion, and

Mosely stirred restlessly.

"That's the way certain people seem to make it out."

There was a long, uneasy silence. "I think," said Coffee, "we better go take a look."

A curiously strained procession of riders now wound its way down the tortuous trail to Split Cañon. Presently the gray ancient bars of the disused corral became visible, then, beyond the bars, the shape of a bony sorrel.

An exclamation burst from Mart Mosely. "That's my horse! If Coffee's brand is on that horse. . . ."

"Wait a minute," said Old Man Coffee. "First let's see this Rocking Chair brand."

He dropped to the ground, crawled through the fence, and caught the horse. He turned the animal, slowly, until the off shoulder was visible to the rest. Then Bat Girard gasped, and Mart Mosely's jaw dropped.

Upon the sorrel hide stood out a single brand, plain and clear, but it was the Feed Box brand of Mosely himself, undoctored and unchanged.

"How come you to look so surprised, Mosely, to see your own horse bearing your own brand?"

"Why, durn it . . . ," Mosely began.

Coffee bore him down. "I'll tell you why. You were scared my testimony would get Billy Johnson off, weren't you? You had to discredit me. So you took this horse of yours, and you took your knife, and you curled your brand to look like my own. Then you had this horse hid near my place, and here he is . . . *but still with your brand.* Surprise is natural."

It took a moment or two for Sheriff Crabtree to digest that.

"But if he done all that, like you say, where is this fake brand you claim he put on?"

"I can explain that, too," said Old Man Coffee. "There aren't but two ways this horse could have come here last night. One way is the trail past my cabin . . . but nobody passed there. The other way means swimming Little Bear Creek. Seems like the fellers that Mosely sent with the horse forgot something . . . a knife-curled brand comes out and is lost altogether as soon as it gets wet. Naturally Mosely didn't know about the fake brand getting spoiled while swimming Little Bear Creek in the dark, and . . . picture his surprise!"

"It's a bale of horse feathers," Mosely sputtered.

"You've got me mixed up," said Pete Crabtree. "Maybe Mosely did fake your brand onto his horse with the view to getting you in trouble, and maybe the fake brand did wash out while swimming the creek, but it don't look like you can prove it, Coffee, so I guess there the matter rests. I'm free to admit," he concluded, "that there's no evidence against you as the thing stands now."

"You'll admit more in a minute," said Coffee. "Mosely, I offer three hundred for this sorrel horse."

"I didn't come up here to trade no. . . ."

The old lion hunter's eyes bored into Mart Mosely like picket pins. "Maybe I want this horse because he carries my memory back," he said. "Maybe that horse looks to me a whole lot like one I knew a few years back, over in the Panhandle . . . a horse with what we called the Hog Eye brand. I offer five hundred."

There was a short silence.

"You think you recognize that horse as from somewhere else?" Crabtree asked.

"It's easy proved if I do," said Coffee. "Leave me remind you something about horse brands. If ever that sorrel horse bore the Hog Eye brand, and later that brand was changed

. . . the original brand will show plain and clear on the inside of the hide, soon as that horse is skinned. Maybe I'm buying this horse because I want to read both sides of his hide!"

"What?" Mart Mosely blustered. "Sell a good horse to have him shot. . . ."

Pete Crabtree suddenly laughed. "That's a hot one," he said. "*You* turn down five hundred dollars? Hell!"

Old Man Coffee chuckled grimly. "It's a pretty pickle now," he told Mosely. "You don't dast sell this horse . . . and you don't dast refuse!" He turned to Sheriff Crabtree. "Yeah, that's right . . . look at him. He's the man you want in place of Billy Johnson, who's going free!"

For a moment Old Man Coffee watched Crabtree as the sheriff studied the face of Mart Mosely. Then the lion hunter relaxed into a satisfied grin.

Pete Crabtree had reached out and possessed himself of Mart Mosely's gun.

Pardon Me, Lady

All up and down the West, I don't suppose I ever saw the beat of Charley Brumbaugh. I have worked stock from Oregon to Arizona, and south of the line into Sonora—all through that high desert country between the Rockies and the Coast Ranges, where the range cattle have gone to, now that they have disappeared from Montana and the Great Plains. And I have seen some very queer characters on horseback. But it still seems to me that Charley Brumbaugh overtops them all.

He was six foot three, and he had one of those kind of overflowing figures, shaped like a Bartlett pear; and we used to say that Charley and the little scrub pony he rode weighed exactly the same to the pound. On top of all this he had a kind of funny, round, square face with curly straw-colored hair, a little snub nose, and a mouth that was plenty ample for him to stick his foot in it. Though, now that I think of it, I suppose Charley hardly ever caught sight of his feet.

But the really grand, magnificent thing about Charley Brumbaugh was his opinion of himself. To hear Charley tell it, he was not only just one huge mass of muscle and the best horseman in the West, but also the most courageous man he had ever seen, and the most intelligent. He was the boy who could tell you how to break the horse, or shoot the wolf, or make love to the girl. I never yet heard anybody ask

Charley for his opinion, and I never yet knew Charley to hold it back.

Once, just once, there was a boy that really took Charley's advice—just deliberately went out and tried to do what Charley suggested. And of all the peculiar things that always seemed to follow Charley Brumbaugh around waiting for a time to happen, this case was the one that really got me down.

This young cowboy, Hugh Kerry, was maybe the last one you'd ever expect to see take any advice from anybody, let alone Charley Brumbaugh. Hugh was still short of twenty years old, and about six foot high, very lean and wiry. The minute you looked him in the eye, which were a blue color, you knew that he was made all in one piece of very good sound stuff. Excessive youngness was really his worst fault, and many of us figured that this would probably be overcome by time.

This youngness often caused Hugh to play a little ahead of himself. He could ride a bronc' right along with any working cowboy, so, of course, he would go to work and get on some contest bucker that had thrown everybody, and he would get bucked down, and blame himself. And that applied to most things he did.

Hugh Kerry had been in a run of this kind of hard luck as we drove our Half Circle D steers up to the loading chutes at Whinrock. What corrals there was for holding stock was already filled up with S Bar Bar cattle from over in the Standing Horse country, so we bedded down alongside the railroad, and the big end of us went on into town.

Hugh Kerry and I went rolling down Whinrock's one little main street, with much loud ringing of spurs, which we had kept on for this purpose, and feeling very much ourselves as cow hands are liable to do when finally they get to town. We hadn't gone very far when Hugh Kerry ran into the little circumstance that doubled him all up.

There were a couple of girls standing on the walk in front of the little hotel, talking. One of them was just about the prettiest girl I had ever set eyes on up to now. It wasn't so much anything in particular, like the color of her eyes and hair, for I'm not real sure I remember such—although right now I see her standing there just as plain as life. Sometimes I hope I will always be able to see her clear in my mind as she stood there then, and sometimes I hope I will plumb forget.

The sun was going down behind the Capitán range, and flooding all the desert with a light the color of pure, free gold in the pan. The world seemed kind of still, resting a moment in all that red-gold light that in a minute would be gone. Something about this girl made it seem like she was the center of all this desert country and all this dimming-out golden light. So that it seemed like she was the one thing we had been looking at for all the long time, when we didn't know just what we was after.

I can't explain it any better than that. But, anyway, I was able to understand it, now that Hugh Kerry was really thrown, two loops and a whop, at first sight of this girl.

"We've got to hunt up a drink," I told him.

"I don't know as I want a drink," Hugh said, for maybe the first time in his life.

"You sick?"

Hugh mumbled and cussed and tried to pass it off, and finally allowed that the average cowhand didn't live right, in *his* opinion. "Who do you reckon she is?" he wanted to know. "I'd give a month's pay to know that one thing."

"Fine," I said. "You be writing out an I.O.U., while I go up and ask her."

But, do you know, he wouldn't let me go within a hundred feet of her, let alone ask her a civil question? So, instead, I asked another feller that was standing around looking like an infester of this Whinrock dump.

"Who is that girl just went in the hotel with that other girl?"

"Don't you know who that is? Why, that's Bernice Scott!"

I turned sad, feeling sorry for Hugh. "You're sure?"

"Do I look dumb?"

"I refuse to answer," I said, "for fear of starting a public disturbance." I went back to Hugh. "We'll now continue our interrupted pursuit of a drink," I told him. "That girl is not for the likes of me, let alone the likes of you. That is no more nor less than the daughter of the Interstate Land and Cattle Company. Her pa owns two million cows."

The wind went out of Hugh Kerry. "I don't believe," he said at last, very humble, "I don't believe I could make much headway with the daughter of the Interstate."

"That," I said, "is a masterpiece of understatement . . . a pure masterpiece."

He didn't take my word for it. He went and talked with the feller I had talked to, and later two other fellers. But they told him the same.

You wouldn't hardly believe how that boy was crumpled up. I never saw a feller so knocked out by just one sight of a girl. He wasn't any good at all the rest of the night. Finally I took him back to camp and rolled him in his bed.

I thought he would be over it by morning. But by light of day he seemed to feel even worse than ever, with no interest in life, or even in breakfast. And Hugh, being so low in his mind, must be the reason for the next misfortune that come snaking through the brush and leaped aboard him, no later than at once.

This morning we were still holding our Half Circle D stock about half a mile away from the shipping pens, which was still being hogged by S Bar Bar cattle. The S Bar Bar cars were already on one of the sidings, and our cars were there, too, but an hour after sunup we couldn't make out any signs that the S Bar Bar was loading, or even figuring on it, and we was held up.

Our boss, Crazy Bob Jackson, had hunted up the S Bar Bar boss in the course of the night to see about this very thing, and Crazy Bob had come back very grouchy, and seemingly empty-handed. So now Crazy Bob rounded up four, five of us, and he told Hugh Kerry to take us over to the S Bar Bar boss and ask if there was anything we could do to help them load.

This S Bar Bar boss was a big, lanky feller, with a big nose stuck slantwise across his face, so that his pan looked very much like the Box Z brand. He was a very crusty sort of jigger. Some way or another, he had got himself appointed a deputy under-sheriff in charge of loading chutes, or some fool thing like that, and on this account he was wearing a .45 swung on his leg. With two exceptions this was the only gun I saw in Whinrock, and it left me very unfavorably impressed with the feller, it seemed so self-whooping and kind of whistle-headed to be wearing a gun just because he had horned in on some little political job. This dizzy jigger's name was Ike Stone.

Hugh Kerry now rode up to this S Bar Bar boss. "Mister Stone," he said, "I wonder could we loan you the lend of these boys here, to kind of help you start to get your loading going?"

Ike Stone—he was standing on the ground drinking a cup of coffee, though it was already half past five in the morning, and the day a quarter gone—he looked Hugh Kerry over very cool and slow, and somewhat insulting. I saw that he was the victim of a hangover that was a beaut'. "Why, you young whippersnapper!" Ike Stone said. "Show me my business . . . huh? Well, you take your so-and-so outfit back to your this-and-that boss, and tell him I'll load when I please and how I please, without no help from you or any other sand apes. Now hightail it out of here, before I take you down and slap you with the flat side of your horse!"

There was a real quiet minute, while it sure looked as if there might come a wailing and gnashing of teeth in the cow business. Then Art Stacker, a red-headed kid with a poker face, he let go a long-drawn snort of distress, and I saw that he was sure going to blow up like a balloon and bust if things didn't change pretty quick so that he could laugh out loud. So I followed his eyes to Hugh Kerry, and it pretty near killed me, too. Hugh was just sitting there dumb-founded, unable to figure out any move, and I never saw such a silly expression on human face, or cow face, either.

After a second or two the other boys caught on, and we all sat there kind of shaking in our saddles, but keeping quiet and our faces straight. As Hugh Kerry just quietly turned his horse and rode away, looking so licked that even his pony had his tail between his legs, we was all glad to turn our horses and follow after, anxious for nothing so much as a chance to laugh out loud without letting on to Ike Stone.

When we got out of Ike Stone's hearing—and also out of hearing Ike Stone, who was shouting remarks after Hugh intended to be funny—Art Stacker began singing a little song. It was a song that Hugh Kerry had been singing just the day before, when we come slashing up to the town, with him all full of oats and high-flying ideas and interest in life.

I'll lick that man,
I'll kiss that girl,
I'll ride that bronc'
And I'll make him whirl!
Come a ti-yi
Hahahahahaha. . . .

Art's voice cracked up, and he let go a crowd of laughter until he like to fell out of the saddle, and his pony blew up, probably with laughter, too, for all I know, and away they went across the flats, the pony bucking and Art cackling so he could hardly stick. All the rest of us followed along, whipping up our ponies side-by-side, and laughing fit to die until we was ashamed of ourselves. All except poor Hugh. He just trailed into camp about as low in his mind as a man could get and so hopeless he just didn't seem to give a hoot any more.

I guess we got our giggles out of our system, for after a while some of the boys began to get curious about what had happened to Hugh to change him so. I had explained to one of the fellers the night before about how Hugh had fell and busted his spirits over a girl he got a look at on the street, only to find out he had fell in love with the Interstate Land & Cattle Company by mistake, and how Hugh had spent the rest of the night trying to sing—"I'm just a poor cowboy and know I done wrong."—but unable to get through any of the verses without being overpowered by the sadness of the song. Maybe I shouldn't have told that about Hugh, but, anyway, this feller now explained it to the others, and, by golly, that set them off again.

The S Bar Bar finally got started loading, but still we waited around all day, and toward night we had kind of wore out the funniness of Hugh's misfortunes and begun to lose interest.

But now Charley Brumbaugh, the outfit's serious thinker, he hitched up his pants and tuned in. Charley was having heavy going as cook, mostly due to it being so difficult for him to reach below his knees, and all the cooking being done on the ground. He had finally got the coffee on the fire by means of puttering around with his cook stick, and he came and stood over Hugh while nature took its course.

"The way I see it," Charley Brumbaugh said, "you got one of these double-jointed problems. You might say it divides into two sections."

"You, too, can get divided in two sections," Hugh told him, "if you pester around me."

"In the first place," said Charley, "you have went to work and got yourself grossly insulted by this here Ike Stone. And, in the second place, the reason you let yourself get done this way, you was low in your mind over you seen a girl. You want to know what I'd do in your case?"

"No," said Hugh.

"Well, then," said Charley, "since you've asked me, I'll tell you. In the first place, I'd go over there and talk to this Ike Stone. 'Ike,' I'd say, 'I have been thinking over them remarks of yours you made this morning, and I've come to the conclusion that they was unfriendly.' Follering which," said Charley, "I'd take his gun away from him and. . . ."

"And shoot yourself," Art suggested.

"And slap his face," Charley corrected him. "Now, most likely, he will pick himself up and make a pass at you."

"That last is a shrewd guess," Art said.

"As soon as he made a pass at me," said Charley, "I'd step in and down this bum with a straight left to the button. The day after John L. Sullivan fought in Carson City, him and me had a few words in a saloon, and he made a pass at me, and I stepped in with a straight left to the button. It laid him just as flat as the shadow of a fried egg."

"Sullivan never was in Carson City," Art said.

"Well, John L. and me took it for Carson City, but, of course, you smarties know best," Charley said. "Now your problem is half solved, Hugh. You have laid out Ike Stone, and that squares that part of it. You know what I'd do then?"

Art Stacker suggested: "You'd make a pass at yourself, avoid it, then step in and lay yourself flat with a straight left to the button."

"I reckon that's supposed to be funny," said Charley.

"Not so funny," said Art, "as useful."

"This girl is really the simplest part of the problem," Charley said, ignoring Art. "What's to stop you from going to town and hunting up this girl again? What's to stop you from going up and speaking to her in a nice way, and making a date with her? If you don't know how to go about it, I can tell you. . . ."

"Hugh hasn't got enough cattle," I said. "He's just about two million head short of even qualifying."

"You figure," Charley asked me with pity, "that a girl related to the Interstate Land and Cattle Company is in need of any cattle?" He turned back to Hugh. "What's a couple of million cattle?" he demanded. "Practically a mere nuisance. You're both human beings, ain't you? What's to stop . . . ?"

"What's to stop the old man from raising hell," I put up

to him, "if he gets back here and finds no eats fixed?"

Charley went to take care of his coffee pot, which was boiling over in a state of abandoned hilarity.

Hugh Kerry sat staring very steadily at Charley's yard-wide back. Pretty soon a kind of crazy gleam came into Hugh's eye, and he began fingering over the knuckles of his left hand. "You know," he said, that crazy gleam coming out plain on the surface, "it would be a very strange thing if that old fool happened to be right. I don't know but what he *is* right."

I walked away in disgust.

When I next noticed Hugh, he was saddling his horse. I walked out and tapped him on the shoulder. "Don't ride off on the lone prairie and shoot yourself yet," I said. "Never shoot yourself on an empty stomach."

"I got work to do," Hugh told me.

All of a sudden a suspicion struck me. "You going to town?"

"Maybe I am," he said. "In a little while, after I see to one other thing."

"Great grief in the foothills!" I said. Already I saw the rest of the answer. "Can it be," I said, "that you don't realize that old Charley Brumbaugh hasn't got enough sense to tell the front end of a horse from the back end of a cow . . . or, for that matter, *vice versa?*"

He looked at me long and steadily with a cold, hard, yet somehow feverish glimmer in his eye. "Every man has a right to be right once in his life," he said. "Even Charley Brumbaugh."

"You mean you're going to deliberately walk up to Ike Stone and slap his face?"

"I take his gun away from him first," said Hugh, "according to the scheduled plan."

"Hell in the desert!" I said. "I got to see this."

I run for my saddle.

Ike Stone had made some headway by fits and starts during the day, but he was still loading his S Bar Bar cattle as we rode up to the chutes. He was sitting on a fence, watching his cowboys haze his cattle around with a lot of noise of whoopings and cows bellowing and hoofs stamping around, and he was looking very black and gloomy, with the smoke of his cigarette mixing with a continual drift of dust from the work and a smell of cows perspiring.

Hugh Kerry dropped off his horse. "Hello, Mister Stone," he said, very cool and level.

Ike Stone turned around and looked at him without any outstanding delight. "Beat it," he said at last, and turned back to looking at the cattle.

Ike Stone's holster had slipped down to where you could see the handle of the gun between two bars of the fence, and Hugh Kerry reached through and got it. He gave the gun a kind of flip, and sent it flying over the cattle train.

Everybody stopped work and stood staring as Ike Stone spun on the top rail to face us.

"Come down here," said Hugh. He grabbed Ike Stone by the ankle and snapped him down off the fence. Ike's boot heels had no sooner hit the ground than Hugh let go with a full swing and slapped Stone's face so hard that Stone's feet seemed to kind of jerk out from under him, and he went down in a kind of reclining position.

But not for long. The boss of the S Bar Bar fairly seemed to bounce, and he come to his feet, cussing a blue streak. His face was near as red as a bay horse, except where you could see Hugh's handprint laid on like whitewash.

What happened then was so quick that it seemed like both men struck at once. As Ike Stone rushed, he let go a long-reaching overhand left that would have downed a horse, if it had hit one, and Hugh ducked in quicker than a greased cat. There was a loud crack that was Hugh sticking out his left and Ike running into it. This time Ike Stone was on his back in the dust, with his knees sticking up crooked, and one hand waving kind of slow and futile in front of his face.

Hugh Kerry turned to the cowboys of the S Bar Bar, who had chosen to take the part of bystanders. "Pour a bucket of water over him," Hugh ordered them, "and, when he comes to, ask him what day it is, and, if so, how does he know?"

With that Hugh swung into his saddle and jog-trotted slowly down the line of the chutes and around the end of the train. He turned his pony toward the town.

"Boy, boy," I said, "that left was a sweetheart! That was every bit as good as the imaginary wallop with which Charley Brumbaugh knocked out John. L. Sullivan."

Hugh shrugged his shoulders. "We'll see how the other half of Charley's advice works out," he said.

"Hugh," I said, "listen to me. You have taken a damn' fool piece of advice . . . maybe the worst and silliest advice I ever heard . . . and through guts and a good straight left, you have somehow made a dumb play stand up. I have no doubt that you are now the hero of the S Bar Bar cowhands, and they will make up a song about you. But let this satisfy you. Get your chin up off the saddle horn, and we'll go back and eat. What do you care if you can't have all the girls in the world?"

"There's only one girl *I* ever took any notice of," Hugh said.

This was not exactly true, but I let it pass.

"Go on back, if you want," he said, and rode on into town.

Naturally we did not find this girl standing in the same place. We hunted up and down the street, looking in stores and around corners. Sundown came, and faded again, and it was dusk. I was trying to tell Hugh Kerry that maybe this girl was imaginary, too, like the achievements of Charley Brumbaugh.

Then, just as he was about to give it up, we sighted her once more, and Hugh froze in his tracks. In the dusk we couldn't see her so good as we had the day before in all that golden light. Yet, even from 'way down the street I would have recognized her out of a thousand, or ten thousand, or at the end of a hundred years. Every move she made set you with the idea that there never had been such a girl before, and never would be again, was you to look forever.

Hugh Kerry's voice brought me out of it. "Good bye, Bill," he said. He turned and stuck out his hand, very sad and solemn, like a man who is about to get shot, or possibly hung.

"Turn back, Hugh," I said, "before you make yourself look like a fool. You have exactly the same chance with this girl as Charley Brumbaugh has!"

"I got to try it, Bill," he said very solemnly. He sounded like a man I once heard use those very same words, just as he was about to jump his horse across a rock split that he must have known his pony couldn't make.

"Well, good bye, Hugh."

"Good bye, Bill." He leaned forward and loped his pony down the street. He run twenty yards past the girl, then turned and walked his pony back, and swung down, alongside. Hugh took off his hat and spoke to her. The girl kind of hesitated, then stopped and answered him.

I sat waiting for Hugh to back away, looking foolish and whipped, and get back on his horse again. But somehow it seemed that there was some delay in this program. Hugh did not get back on his horse right away. It must have been three or four minutes while Hugh and the girl stood there talking, and all the time I was getting more restless, and kind of nervous, feeling that something was wrong.

Then, dog-gone it, the strangest thing happened yet. I couldn't believe my eyes. I couldn't hear what they was saying to each other, but now I heard the girl laugh, and I saw Hugh begin to kind of grin. After a minute more, I'll be darned if the two of them didn't turn and stroll off down the street—absolutely arm in arm!

I stared after them, and so did my horse, and so did Hugh's horse. Me and the two horses, representing three nonplused ninnies, not one of us understanding any more about this thing than another. Finally I reached up and pushed my mouth shut and climbed down off my horse and went in the Elite Café.

An hour later, when I come out, Hugh's horse was still there.

Charley Brumbaugh had been bad enough with his bragging and his tall stories and his free advice before this thing happened, and now that somebody had actually carried out his advice, and not only that, but it had worked, I naturally thought there would not be any living with old Charley any more.

But, do you know, it took exactly the opposite effect? When Charley heard this story about Hugh licking the matter and walking off with the girl, at first he couldn't believe it. Finally, when it soaked in, he was stunned. He started to say: "Why, naturally . . . didn't I tell . . . ?" But he was pale around the gills, and his voice trailed off. That night Charley was very quiet, and looking upset and scared. All the next day he still was not himself. Finally, by the end of the day, Charley quit and faded off on the caboose of the cattle train.

Nobody could understand why the success of his advice had took this effect on Charley. But do you know what I think? All the time Charley Brumbaugh was giving advice, and telling about the hero he let on to be, he was living in an imaginary world of his own, unmarred by any actual facts. And finally, when somebody really took his advice and made it work—why, it was just like as if reality had busted into his imaginary world—and it come near scaring him to death!

Maybe I should have spared Charlie Brumbaugh this dismay. Maybe I should have told him why it was his advice had worked, and Hugh had been able to gather up this uncatchable girl.

You see, after Hugh had walked off with the girl and I went in the Elite Café to pull myself together, I found myself sitting at the counter beside the same denizen of Whinrock who had told me who this girl was in the first place.

"Cowboy," he said, "you look dumbfounded."

"I'm not only dumbfounded, I'm flabbergasted," I admitted. "You know that kid cowpuncher that was with me yesterday?"

"Seems like I recall him."

"Well, sir," I told him, "you'll call me a liar. But that boy just picked up and walked off with Bernice Scott . . . the daughter of all the Interstate Land and Cattle!"

"When? Now?"

"Within the five minutes. I seen it with my own eyes."

"No," said the Whinrock resident. "No, you never. Because Bernice Scott and her father left Whinrock this morning."

"Look here," I said. "You, yourself pointed that girl out to me as Bernice Scott."

"There was two girls there," he reminded me. "I thought you meant the important one. The good-looking one is some girl that waits on table, over there at the hotel."

Six-Gun Graduate

Johnny Everett had never interested himself in gunfighting until they woke him up, that night in Lost Creek, to tell him that Sandy had gotten himself killed by Doc Regan. Yet he reached for his gun belt instantly, instinctively, at the word. Sandy had been Johnny Everett's partner for going on three weeks, ever since they had fallen into company on the long lonely trail into the Standing Rocks. And, since they had been in the mining camp of Lost Creek but eighteen hours, Sandy had no other friend. Now that Sandy was dead, it did not occur to Johnny that it was possible to let the matter rest.

Then, because Johnny was no fool, second thought came to him. Johnny had never been in a gunfight in his life. Doc Regan was known as a crack gunfighter from the Madres to the Cinnabars. Putting two and two together, Johnny saw that before he killed Doc Regan there would have to be some changes made. That was how Johnny Everett got started in that extraordinary, dogged study of his. From that hour he was in training to kill a man.

He loaded Sandy's horse with grub and all the cartridges his money would buy, and headed out of town. Someone had told him where to find an unused cabin in the lonely hills. Here, a day's ride from Lost Creek, Johnny off-saddled, set up a row of tin cans, and settled himself to the long job of preparing to kill Doc Regan.

It was slow work at first, while he was alone. At the end of the fourth day he was discouraged to find that a slightly lamed wrist and a blister on his thumb were about all he had to show. Then the fifth day Johnny got his break. A tall man with a rifle over his arm was standing at the edge of the timber as Johnny turned away from knocking over the day's first row of tin cans. "I was kind of figuring to lay over here," Johnny's visitor said. "But if I'll be bothering you, I'll be on my way."

"You won't be bothering me," Johnny said.

"Mind if I watch?"

"Sure not."

The stranger preserved an hour's silence. Perhaps he never would have interfered at all, if Johnny had not asked him how the gun work looked. "Why," the visitor evaded, "do you hook your thumb in your belt just before you go for your gun?"

"Say, look here," Johnny said. "You know anything about this gunfighting?"

"A little."

Johnny Everett considered. "I had a partner killed on me a few days ago," he said at last. "A man can't leave it lie. But I'm terrible. If you got any time to spare, I'd sure like to hear your guess on what I'm doing wrong."

The other seemed interested and pleased. "I don't mind laying over a couple of days," he said. "My name's Bill." And right there Johnny really began to learn a thing or two.

Instead of laying over two days, Bill camped with Johnny a week, then a second week, then a third. He worked with Johnny casually the first day or two, but later he set himself at it in good earnest. Johnny told him one afternoon that it was Doc Regan he meant to kill.

"That's bad medicine, boy," said Bill. "The West is full

of fellers that cut their teeth on a gun butt. But not one in a thousand has the natural ability to make a gunfighting name."

"I'm not setting out to make a name," said Johnny. "When I've killed Regan, I'm through killing."

"If you kill Doc Regan, you'll have only begun. Every drunk that wants to prove he's bad will get to thinking what a feather in his cap it would be to kill the man that killed Regan. You'll be a marked man, son, and you'll never get loose from it."

For a moment Johnny wondered if it would be possible for him to go his way and forget Regan. But he shook his head. "I can't help myself."

Bill shrugged. "That's up to you."

As the days passed, Bill seemed to forget his own plans utterly—whatever they had been—in devotion to his pupil's progress. Bill was a great instructor. He was more than a six-gun enthusiast—guns were his passion, his life.

At the end of a month Bill concluded that he had done all for Johnny he could. Johnny's natural wince at the roar and shock of the gun was gone; his draw was quick and smooth. It was time for Johnny to go.

"You work pretty good," Bill admitted, when at last, on a cold gray morning, Johnny saddled to go down after his man. "You'd kill any ordinary man."

"Bill," Johnny said, "tell me one thing . . . why did you spend all this time and trouble on me?"

Bill's grin was half sheepish. "Aw, well, shucks . . . I just kind of got interested, I guess."

"I sure appreciate it, Bill." Johnny hesitated. He felt that something had been left unsaid, and he couldn't remember what it was. "Well . . . wish me luck . . . I'll be going now."

"Sure, Johnny." They shook hands. "But you don't

need to go any place."

"Huh?"

"I'm Bill Regan."

"You mean you're Doc Regan?"

"They call me that."

Johnny stared at him a long time, and his face went red, then white again. All his established order of things seemed to go up in the air like a sun-fishing bronc', but he rallied. The man before him was no longer the patient Bill, but the man he had trained himself to kill. His voice rose high and strained, so that it cracked in the middle. "Why you . . . you damned. . . ." His gun came into his hand.

It was a good draw Johnny made, smooth and quick, well taught and well practiced. But he never saw just how Doc Regan drew. One gun crashed, and Johnny Everett was swaying on his legs, staring idiotically at the blood that was running down his empty hand.

Through this fog of shock he heard Doc Regan's hard, grim voice: "There's one more lesson, you little fool. And I'd give ten thousand dollars if somebody had given me the like!"

Range Bred

Las Cruces, little old cow town though it was, always drew a good crowd for its rodeo. Today the crowd was a whopper. It overflowed the grandstand, and pressed a thin dense line of people around the whole circle of the wire that hemmed the arena. Because the crowd was never entirely still, the younger of the forty or fifty cow-country riders within the dusty ten acres found it hard to forget that they were in the focus of ten thousand eyes. But the old contest hands lounged nonchalantly in their saddles or on the chute gates, indifferent to the impersonal crush outside.

The announcer's voice was blaring out over the loud-speakers: "Chute number five. . . . Pete Reese of Tucson, coming out on the next bucking horse."

Behind the bars of chute number five the red shadow-striped shape of a bronc' named Murdershot jerked and heaved as the bucking strap clinched on his flanks, and his hoofs battered the planking. The forty or fifty riders—mostly cowboys, but with a scattering of girls—were the crack ropers and bronc' men of five states. Many of them had witnessed a thousand rodeo events, but they were quiet now, almost to a man, watching the saddling chutes. Knowing their game, they knew things about Murdershot that the crowd did not.

Murdershot was from up back of the Pipe Rock country—he had never felt rope until he was five years old—and he had been in the man-fighting game only a little time. Before he had got on Jake Hutchinson's contest string, he had been saddled perhaps half a dozen times, and sometimes ridden and sometimes not, but that was without the flanker—the thin strap rigged behind the cantle and cruelly cinched so that the fighting bronc' went wild and bucked beyond himself, kicking at the moon.

In the few times he had been contested, something had always been wrong—he had smashed his rider's knee against the chute gate; he had popped a cinch; he had fallen and crippled his rider. Nobody knew yet whether the horse could be ridden or not, under rodeo rules. But every rider who had seen the red outlaw in action had him marked as a bucker who would be famous, in another year.

This was the unknown quantity that Pete Reese of Tucson was now about to ride—or try to. Pete Reese was a tall youngster made of whalebone and rawhide, and his face was weather-tanned leather. The riders, lounging in their saddles, waited in silence to see what he would do.

Of them all, not one waited with a more watchful attention than Glory Austin, who sat near the chutes on a borrowed buckskin pony. Unless you were a horseman you might not have noticed her there, a slim, straight-sitting girl in black broadcloth and silk. Her soft dust-colored hair and her cleanly made, olive-tanned features, heavily shadowed by her broad-brimmed hat, did nothing to make her conspicuous. Even if you had been near, her heavy-lashed gray eyes might have failed to catch your attention, for there were gates behind them that were closed to you and me.

Glory Austin was not entered in the bronc' riding; her own trick riding work was done for the day, and done well. With the money won, she should have felt relaxed and comfortably weary. But with Pete Reese about to ride, she waited with sharp attention.

Glory Austin had known Pete Reese only a space of months, but she had known the first time she had seen him that he was one in ten thousand—perhaps one in the world—so far as she was concerned. But for another reason this ride was, to Glory Austin, different from any other Pete Reese had ever made. Glory had never seen the red horse Murdershot until today, but if anybody could read the whole soul of a range-bred horse just by looking at him, Glory could. And she had recognized that Murdershot had been foaled to make a name as a killer. She did not believe it was by accident that Murdershot had somersaulted himself onto his rider at Cheyenne.

The announcer's loudspeaker was bawling: "Pete Reese is about to come out now. . . . He's easing into the saddle. . . . One of the boys is up on the chute to give a last hand on the flank strap."

Lois Bart, Glory Austin's partner—they pooled and split their winnings—put her horse alongside Glory's. Lois Bart had a mop of red hair, and she wore a green silk shirt and a gold-filigreed belt to set it off; her flair for the spectacular made her a striking figure in any man's arena.

"It'll be a hot one on Pete," Lois offered now, "if that broomtail dumps him." She chuckled. "I'm sure crazy about that man. But maybe a good spin on his neck might do him good!"

Glory Austin said nothing. For a moment she wondered what had ever persuaded her to go partners with this girl, so different from herself. Then she forgot Lois as the gate swung.

"Here he comes!" A galvanized silence held everywhere for an instant as Murdershot gathered himself, whirled, and shot into the open blast of the sun.

Glory's trained eye saw the savage twist of the tall red bronc' as he slammed into his pitch. Murdershot leaned low to the ground, and zigzagged, snapping himself like a quirt. Pete Reese himself was almost unseated on the second jump. On the third and fourth jumps he was fighting to stay with the horse.

Although the horse had as good as lost him with those terrific side-whipping snaps, Glory saw that Pete was raking Murdershot with his tape-covered rowels—raking him high and handsome every jump. Murdershot bawled—the throaty scream of a fighting horse crazy with anger—and the crowd began to roar, for Pete still rode. Ten seconds end an official ride, and now the whistle screamed, signaling in the pick-up men.

It was the job of the pick-up men to swing Pete out of the saddle. Ordinarily it is not a hard job for a practiced man to pick up the rider, but with this horse it was different. He was halfway down the field now, and his erratic twistings made it tough for the pick-up horses. Jack Evers, hazing on the right, jammed his pony in close.

Murdershot whirled in mid-buck, stood on his head, and his heels smashed out at the hazing horse. Jack Evers's horse staggered, and stood still, quivering. Jack was sitting with his head down, half doubled up in the saddle.

Murdershot's whirl had changed his course, and Jack's pick-up partner on the other side of the bronc' was caught as he closed to make his try. Murdershot cannoned broadside into the pick-up pony. The pick-up horse and rider went down.

For once in Glory's life a horse had her afraid. She was obsessed by the idea that Murdershot would not be satisfied with losing his man, but would stop and trample him. The red horse was insane, crazy in the manner of a fighting wolf—his smash at Jack Evers showed that.

Glory did not realize that she, also, was racing down the field, her pony hovering on the heels of the bronc', until Lois's voice reached her from behind, frantic with warning: "Glory, you fool, stay out!"

Glory did not stay out. There were other horses coming up, but the nearest on her side was fighting his head and his rider, and now there opened for Glory a brief opportunity. It wasn't a big chance, and it involved no heroism. It was just one of those split-second chances in which a rider can bring a hard-earned skill to bear in the moment in which it is most needed.

Glory cut in fast, spurring her buckskin pony against the flank of the red bucker. She was not trying for the rider, but for the flank-strap buckle, sure from long experience that Murdershot would straighten out, once he was free of the biting flanker. She leaned far out and grabbed at the loose end of the strap.

Murdershot swung away, half dragging her from the saddle, then surged back, his heels smashing at Glory's pony. The buckskin staggered, as Jack Evers's horse had done a few seconds before, and the break jerked in Glory's teeth. But the flank strap was cut loose.

The worst of the crazy fight went out of Murdershot suddenly. He bucked still, but a new rider coming in on the left—Tom Hansen this time—was able to close in. Hansen picked Pete out of the saddle. Pete swung across the rump of Hansen's horse, and was on the ground.

Glory pulled up, and sat breathing deeply on her shaking pony. She saw Pete Reese on his feet, looking around as if uncertain where his ride had taken him.

"It put two men out of business," Tom Hansen said, "getting you off that pony. Somebody cut loose the flanker

. . . or, by golly, you'd be on him yet!"

"Who threw that flank strap off?" Pete demanded.

Lois Bart had ridden in between Glory and Pete Reese. Now she turned to Glory, and winked. "I did," she said.

That was the way it always was, always had been ever since Glory and Lois had thrown in together as partners. If there was any scrap of credit to be had, it went to Lois Bart, now and always. As presently Pete Reese, also, would belong to Lois.

Glory Austin rode back to the chutes slowly, alone. She had returned the buckskin pony to the cowboy who had lent it to her and was turning away, when Rowdy Kate Hutchinson came up, clamped a mighty hand on her shoulder, and walked her away from the other riders. Big old Kate had long ago ended her own riding days, but she had married a bucking-horse string. Her bass-voiced bellowings were esteemed necessary to half the rodeos of the West—as necessary as her broad, towering figure, with its battered hat and rough clothes.

"Honey, are you hurt?" Kate asked.

"I'm not hurt!"

"The hell you ain't!" Old Rowdy Kate was rough and noisy, but she babied the rodeo girls. "The trouble with you Austins, you ain't willing to let on you're human. You sure ain't much like your partner. I've known Lois Bart to leave herself be carried out of the arena. . . . right past the grandstand, of course. . . . when I couldn't find a scratch on her. And here's another thing! The next time you trick ride a rodeo, I want to see. . . ."

"I'm through with rodeos," Glory said.

"What's this, now?"

Glory Austin flared up surprisingly. "I'm through, and I'm through for good. I'm sick of the whole business! I don't care if I never see a rodeo again."

"Why, child, what's got into you?"

"It's show-off!" Glory said fiercely. "I was born and raised on the working ranges, and I don't know anything except horses, and that's what pulled me into the rodeo game. But the crowds, and the everlasting making a show of it . . . that spoils it all!"

"All of us come from the working range," Rowdy Kate pointed out. "Where else would a body learn to ride?"

"That's just it," Glory said. "The riding and roping is honest and real. But this showmanship stuff makes a sham of the whole thing."

Rowdy Kate studied her in some bewilderment. "Too much Lois Bart," Kate decided. "And on top of that, you're gone on Pete Reese, that's the trouble with you! Don't go trying to kid me, either . . . I know. He started working on you 'way back in the middle of last season, the first time he ever seen you. And he could have scooped you in easy as dabbing a rope on you . . . or you him, if you'd known it. Then you threw in with this Lois Bart, and she sets right to work prying him loose."

"They don't make 'em like Pete," Glory said steadfastly.

"Let me tell you this . . . the rider don't live that's worth a good snap in the pants with a romal! I know, honey . . . I know."

Glory said: "It isn't true Pete blows his money on toots in old Mex'. Mexico gets his money, all right, but it's land and cattle it goes into."

"I expect you and I are about the only ones know that, honey," Kate agreed. "The kid'll be a big man in the Southwest someday . . . or sure would . . . if your belief in him counted in the score. About the pick of the crop, such as it is. But I'm sorry you're gone on him so."

Glory Austin surrendered; you couldn't hide anything from old Kate. "I can't help it, Kate."

"I know." Rowdy Kate had watched riders come and go. She had known a hundred Lois Barts before now, and perhaps one or two other Glory Austins. Glory's father had been a cattle king. Kate perceived in the girl a valid aristocracy, of a kind never known to any other country than this Western country—an aristocracy of thousand-mile ranges, dusty, bellowing herds, and wild horses.

Yet Kate understood how the spectacular, free-and-easy Lois Bart could rope and tie a whole parade of men—or even take a man away from Glory Austin. Behind Glory's eyes gray gates could close. But Lois Bart's eyes were different—warm, sidelong eyes, and behind them were no gates, at all.

"Men are all saps," Kate said, "and that little hooker is too fast for you, kid."

Glory did not seem to hear. "I've got to get out of this. I can't ever forget him, Kate, if I keep seeing him around."

"Maybe," Kate admitted moodily, "that would be the best thing. Though if it was me. . . ." She broke off abruptly.

The color had gone out of Glory's face again, and Kate could make out the hoof scar on the tough black broadcloth below Glory's knee—it had a wet look. Kate rapped the top of Glory's half-boot with the butt of her quirt. Glory flinched, and the leg gave under her.

"Uhn-huh," Kate said, holding her up. "I knew I seen that bronc' whale you. Prob'ly split wide open!" Kate swept an arm under Glory's knees and picked her up.

"Let me down! I tell you I'm. . . ."

"Yeah, you're all right. You told me that already." Kate shouldered her way out the riders' gate. "Now, will you shut your fool head, or will I bust you one?"

Glory Austin walked into rodeo headquarters that evening trying hard not to favor the leg Murdershot had kicked. There were seven stitches in that leg, and from knee to boot heel the whole thing seemed numb except for the aching beat of the pulse, but she wouldn't limp.

Tomorrow would be the second of the three days, and one of the exhibition features would be a special ride by one of the girls on a horse that had distinguished itself the first day. Whoever wanted the ride had to draw for the horse tonight, and it was like drawing for money, for twenty-five dollars went with the ride, scratch, grab, or thrown, with seventy-five dollars more if the ride qualified.

The girl who rode would have her stirrups hobbled out of their free swing, making it easier to stay, and there would be no flank strap. Under these conditions Jake Hutchinson had named Murdershot as the logical horse.

Rodeo headquarters had been set up in Billy Weston's saddle shop. When the rodeo people were gathered there, they overflowed down the little frame structure. Just now, though, a big dance was going on over at Miners' Hall, and nearly all the riders were over there—including Pete Reese. Jake Hutchinson was here, however, with Rose Moran, a buxom girl who rode the bronc's by main strength, and Bess Oliver, a dark, hawk-faced girl, flat and hipless as a cowboy.

"Where's Lois Bart?" Jake asked. "Glory, are you going to draw for Lois?"

"I don't run Lois Bart," Glory said. "Go ahead and put her in the draw, if you want. I figure to draw for myself."

"That isn't right," Bess Oliver contended hotly. "Glory and Lois is partners, and they split the money. Why should they get two draws for their money, and we all get one?"

"I don't know anything about that," said Jake. "This is the way we always done it."

As it turned out, it made no difference. Glory Austin drew Murdershot, as somehow she had known she would.

Three cowboys tried to date her for the evening before she got away. She turned them down.

She went back to her room at the edge of town. Most of the rodeo people booked space in the hotels, but, in Las Cruces, Glory was always taken in by a half-Mexican woman who had once worked for Glory's mother. The old adobe was clean and unpretentious; its little windows looked out upon the desert.

Lois Bart had not come in. In her cool room, faintly lighted by an old-fashioned hand lamp, Glory Austin suddenly felt terribly alone. Until there was nothing to do but go to bed with the ache of her injury. She had not realized how much she had hoped to meet Pete down at headquarters.

She went to bed and allowed herself to weep a little, until the breeze off the desert brought her the far-off whimper of a coyote. Then she felt better, and presently went to sleep.

Lois Bart came in at two o'clock, exuberant and noisy. Glory was sitting up by the time Lois had lighted the lamp.

That old adobe room was kind to Glory Austin, unkind to Lois Bart. In the yellow kerosene light Lois looked tired and a little hard. But Glory Austin, with her soft dust-colored hair about her shoulders, had the glow of soft platinum and old gold. In this room she was a different, soft-lined, white-shouldered Glory—a Glory such as Pete Reese had never seen.

"Where was you?" Lois demanded. "Pete Reese hauled me to the dance."

"Well, of course, Lois. I never yet knew you to miss a throw of your loop."

Lois Bart grinned and stretched luxuriously, shaking out her red hair. "Pete'll be all right, once I get shoes on him," she said. "Can I help it if he runs after me? What do you care?"

"I don't care."

"Say, I heard you drew me that Murdershot ride. That's swell! I can ride that bronc' from. . . ."

"You heard wrong," said Glory.

"Huh? Why, Rose Moral said you talked Jake Hutchinson into letting both our names in the hat, and you drew. . . ."

"I drew Murdershot for myself."

"For yourself? Say, you don't want to ride Murdershot!"

"That's the way the draw went."

"Draw? Since when have they made a rule against swapping draws? We're partners, ain't we? I'll ride that. . . ."

"I think," said Glory, "you'll do nothing of the kind."

Lois Bart changed her tactics. "Look here, Glory. I'm not saying you can't ride. You can take a tough broomtail and make a good Indian of him quicker than anybody can. But this rodeo riding is different. There's no use. . . ."

"Don't worry about splitting the hundred," Glory said. "I'll qualify, all right."

"It isn't that. I heard you got hurt this afternoon. I heard you had to have your leg sewed up."

"A little hoof cut isn't anything," Glory said stubbornly.

"Glory, it isn't fair! That isn't what we agreed to when we went partners. I'm supposed to do the bronc' riding, and you're supposed to do the other stuff. What will people say if . . . ?"

"You're worrying about missing a chance to astonish Pete Reese," Glory said disgustedly.

"Well, maybe I am," Lois admitted. "I'm the one that can make a show of it, ain't I?"

They argued while Lois was dressing, and they still argued after the light was out, Glory sticking doggedly to her right to make the ride. But in the end it was Glory who gave in. She gave in because she was weary and disgusted, and the kick Murdershot had given her hurt miserably, but mostly because she was sick of the whole policy of show-off that was Lois Bart's stock in trade. She had begun to see the motive behind her own stubbornness for what it was—which was nothing more than a desire to make a flash ride for Pete's benefit.

"Take the horse and ride him to hell and back, if you can," she said at last.

"Atta-girl!"

To win second-day money in the trick riding took everything Glory Austin had. After it was over, she found it so hard to dismount that she feared she would stumble and go down if she tried it. So she sat her lather-splashed pony near the chutes, waiting for the hammering in her hurt leg to ease. It was time for Lois Bart to make her ride. Murdershot was already in the chute, and the announcer's loudspeaker was blaring: "Yesterday you saw Murdershot fight a good man to a standstill. Today. . . ."

With her eyes set on the distance, trying to make sure that her head was going to stay clear until the effect of her hard riding had worn off, Glory Austin did not see Pete Reese come up until he was at her stirrup.

Pete's height made her feel as if she were on an undersized pony, which she was not. As he looked up at her, she had a sudden impulsive desire to let herself keel out of the saddle into his arms. But she sat stiffly, poker-faced.

"Say, look here," Pete said. "I heard you got hurt yesterday. What kind of fraud is that?"

The gray gates closed behind Glory Austin's eyes. "Just one of those rumors, Pete."

"I knew that," he said, "when I saw you trick ride. You sure rode like a streak! But last night I kind of worried. I looked all over for you."

"I was well hid," Glory said. "I was at rodeo headquarters."

"Well, I missed you, then. This morning, after I heard you'd given Lois your Murdershot ride, I thought you must be hurt for sure."

"Well, we figured Lois could do better with it than I could."

"I never heard such bunk," said Pete. "You can outride Lois or any other girl that ever saddled a bronc', and you know it. I'll say more than that . . . you can outride me, or any man."

"I wouldn't last long on Murdershot, I guess."

"If you couldn't, nobody could." Glory said nothing, and after a moment Pete went on: "Still, I don't know. I don't blame you for shying off of Murdershot. I don't trust him much."

"You don't blame me for . . . what?"

"Shucks, I'm afraid of that horse myself. Seems like the flanker puts him clean out of his head. If you were coming out on the bronc' with a flank strap, I'd sure raise hell. Don't know but what I would anyway."

Glory Austin demanded outright: "Pete, you think I'm afraid of that bronc'?"

"Sure not, child! But anybody has a right to be. I'm afraid of him myself."

Glory looked away. She didn't notice that one of the judges was shouting for Pete, or that he moved away, until she looked around for him and he was gone. A crazy notion was hammering into her head, beating upward from the mark Murdershot had put on her. Pete Reese thought that she was afraid—afraid to ride the red bronc', with no flanker and hobbled stirrups. The notion hurt worse than the wound.

For a moment Glory Austin felt infinitely discouraged and a little sick. It seemed to her then that nobody understood anything she did, ever, and never would. Then abruptly her temper broke.

Glory Austin's temper was slow in starting, but now it snapped as if a cartridge had exploded in her head. It suddenly came over her that she had stood enough from Lois Bart and Pete Reese and rodeos, and from them all. And all in a moment she went crazy mad. She spurred the steel-dust pony close against chute number five, where Murdershot stood. She dismounted on the run, and, although she winced and dropped to one knee as her weight came upon her hurt leg, she recovered instantly.

Lois ran up, shouting: "See they get that hull screwed down right, will you, Glory? I got to see the announcer!"

Glory said: "I'll take care of it, all right." She was poker-faced, but there was a blaze behind her eyes as she turned to the chutes.

Lois went running down the chutes to the announcer's stand. That was an old trick of hers—at the last minute she was always on hand with some gag for the announcer to give out, with a little extra publicity to her name as a rodeo girl.

Lois Bart's saddle was already on Murdershot, and the stirrups would be, too, but there was no time to change that now. Glory ran a quick eye along the chutes. Nearby loitered a big Indian bulldogger.

Glory called sharply: "José! *¡Aqui!*"

José responded with alacrity, and Glory spoke under her breath, in Spanish. "Get up on that chute, and let that flanker down!" She inspected the cinch and saw that the handlers had already whipped it tight. She snapped her knife open, and, reaching under the red horse through the bars, she slashed through the stirrup hobbles, so that both stirrups swung free and clear. She reached under for the flank strap and passed the end up to José, then climbed the chute.

Tom Hansen, who had cinched Lois Bart's saddle on Murdershot, suddenly woke up. "Here, what are you doing? Lois don't want any flanker! Lois said. . . ."

Glory Austin eased into the saddle. "To hell with Lois Bart! I drew this horse, and I'm riding him!" She spoke over her shoulder to José. "Give him the flanker," she said between her teeth. "Cut him in two . . . you hear me?"

José heaved upward, and the flank strap smoked through its buckle, biting deep as the big Indian almost lifted Murdershot off the ground. The red horse slammed his heels into the planking, and half reared in the chute. Glory Austin shouted: "Swing that gate!"

The man on the gate rope was Shorty Ferris, naturally a pop-eyed little man, but immensely more so now. "Hey, look . . . wait a minute! I thought. . . ."

Glory did not know where Rowdy Kate came from, but suddenly she was there beside the chute. "If Glory says open it," Rowdy Kate bellowed, "damn it, you open it, you little squirt!"

The gate swung. With the flank strap a good six hundred pounds tight, the stirrups unhobbled, Glory Austin came out on Murdershot.

For an instant then, as Murdershot went into his first savage twisting plunge, Glory realized what she had done. For just an instant she glimpsed herself in cool perspective—a girl rider with one leg half useless, who had gone crazy mad long enough to put herself on an outlaw that the best of the men could hardly hope to stay with, and she knew that she was a fool.

The next instant she was fighting as if for her life—perhaps in truth fighting for her life, for all she knew. It seemed to her that the first rocketing twist and shock as good as broke her back. But she set her teeth hard and swung both spurs high and free, raking Murdershot's neck, left side, right side, and left again.

The horizon pitched crazily. On her left, the sun-blasted earth swung up suddenly so near and close that she flung out her arm to save the impact, then abruptly the earth dropped away again, and somehow she had stayed. In the instant that she was upright she snapped off her hat and threw it downward at Murdershot's pinned-back ears with all her strength, then swung her spurs high to rake him again—left side, right side, high, loose, and handsome.

The arena was reeling, and the earth was reeling. Murdershot screamed like a trumpet. On her right the hazy form of a rider drifted close, then suddenly shot backwards out of sight as the earth whirled. For an instant she glimpsed the face of Pete Reese close to her on her left. Pete's face was curiously expressionless, but his eyes for once were not laughing. She felt his fingers streak across her back as he tried to pick her up and missed.

Glory Austin's breath caught and strangled in her throat

as Murdershot snapped her as if he would jerk out her life. She could not ride this horse. The smashing impacts were sending her blind and dazed, and she reeled to the twists.

Blindly she scratched Murdershot's neck once more, high and handsome, because Pete was there, and it was not true that she was afraid. Then the whole world upset, and, although saddle and horse seemed still between her knees, the flat earth struck upward mightily, and that was the end.

Glory Austin said dimly: "I shouldn't have done that."

"I'll say you shouldn't," said Rowdy Kate.

Glory could see the sunlight now, and she recognized the smell of hay. She could make out the figures of cowboys standing nearby. It was several minutes before she could decide that she was on some hay bales back of the bronc' corrals.

"I shouldn't have done it," said Glory again. "Lois could have rode him. She could have rode him, and got her split of a hundred. In place of just the twenty-five."

"You get the hundred, so far as that goes," said Rowdy Kate. "Your hoss let go all holts and somersaulted . . . but that was after the whistle blowed."

"I kind of figured that was a bad horse," Glory said.

"You figured right! Murdershot jumped up and whirled on you, but Pete Reese drove his hoss head-on into Murdershot, and both hosses went down, then, when the dust cleared, Pete was sitting on Murdershot's head."

"Pete's a good boy," Glory said. "They don't make 'em like Pete any more."

Pete's voice said: "Glory, you mean that?"

" 'Course to hell, she don't mean it," said Kate angrily. "She's out of her head. Now, you clear out of here, you bum! I'm going to tote her over to my car and take her back to town."

"I'll tote her myself," said Pete.

"Who says you will?" Lois Bart cut in. "Kate and I. . . ."

"Go chase yourself," said Pete shortly. "Where's your flivver, Kate?"

Pete Reese rode into town with them, to make sure Glory didn't go out again, and fall off the back seat.

"By God," Pete said when they were halfway back to town, "I'll kill the Indian that put that flank strap on. If ever I find out who cut loose those stirrup hobbles. . . ."

Glory said: "I cut loose those hobbles."

"Dear God," Pete whispered. "It serves me right for letting you get anywhere near that red devil in the first place."

"I'd like to know," Glory said, "what business it is of yours what I ride?"

Pete said with surprising gentleness: "Now, you wait. You listen here to me."

Glory flared up at him. "I don't want to listen to you. I won't listen to you! You can go to hell, Pete Reese!"

The bronc' fighter studied her, looking square into her eyes.

Glory Austin tried to close the gray gates, but she could not. She closed her eyes and began to cry softly, plumb whipped.

For a moment Pete sat motionless, mystified and baffled. Then he gathered her up and held her gently.

This girl in his arms was the other Glory—not the straight-sitting, black-clad figure of saddles and bronc's, but the Glory of the old adobe house: a slim, soft-lined girl, too finely and gently drawn to be used for smashing about in arenas for the amusement of crowds. Perhaps she was born to the open-country aristocracy of vast herds. Perhaps she was steadfast and game, and could herself put mastery on a wild-bred horse. But mostly she was just a bucked-down girl with tears on her cheeks and her hair whipped loose about her throat—a girl someone should have taken better care of.

Pete said: "This show-off stuff isn't for you and me. There's better things for us, in a different kind of place."

Glory smiled faintly, comfortable in his arms.

West of Nowhere

Joe Sebring, piloting a huge-engined gadget with a shape like a clipped-wing bee, found out what he wanted to know in less than ten minutes of flight. He slipped back into the field like a diving kite, and used up three-fourths of the long runway before he dared go to his brakes.

When he had got her stopped, he pushed up his goggles and rubbed his eyes, dog-tired and disgusted. His engine still needed a lot of work before he could take off in the East-to-West—if he was going to race at all. Forty-four hours before take-off it looked very doubtful. He felt as if he had been quarreling continuously with a cranky, flown-out engine for the last sixty-five or seventy years, and that his own age was about a hundred, instead of his actual twenty-two.

Joe had an idea that if the inspectors knew as much about his ship as he knew himself, they would snatch its license. He had rebuilt it out of a total crack-up he had bought for coffee money. He had an engine in it out of a different crack-up. And ship and engine were pulled into a struggling compromise by a propeller not intended for either one. It had taken all winter and part of the summer to get the thing approved.

Yet he knew that this group of misfits would fly like a streak. He had raced it once, and won once, taking the tough Border-to-Border, for an average of one hundred percent. That was many months ago. Since then he had spent most of his time trying to get his airplane in shape to repeat. Sometimes it looked as if the tired old engine had already given its all.

Joe had not started out to be a race pilot. He didn't want to be a race pilot now. But he wasn't eligible for the airlines because he didn't have enough blind time, or any other kind of time, nor the money to get it. Until he had won the Border-to-Border, he had been just one of a large order of young pilots coming up the hard way. Perhaps his single victory could have been made to open up some sort of an opportunity for him, but Joe had a special, stubborn reason for wanting to race again—and wished he had never heard of it.

At the apron of hangar two, however, Ellen Scott walked out to the stubby wing of his ship, and he swung down, grinning. He didn't want her to know that only tenacity was keeping his entry in. As soon as he smiled, he looked about half his age—one of the penalties of being snub-nosed and freckled, but his hands, as he now pulled off his gloves, were broad, square, and stubborn, and ingrained with engine oil.

"Joe," Ellen Scott said, "that motor sounds like a basket of beer cans falling down cellar."

Ellen Scott had a fast plane of her own and got around the country a good deal, but, until yesterday, Joe Sebring had not seen her for a long time. Yesterday, when he had rifled under the power lines with a dead engine, she had walked down the line of hangars to see who the attempted suicide was. She had stayed to spend a couple of hours, watching Joe's work with a sort of absent-minded fascination.

Today she had come back to turn his prop for him while

he checked his timing, and had got a stocking-run out of it. Now she guided a wing as his plane was rolled into the hangar. Nobody else had noticed that Joe Sebring was in the race, and, although this was more than all right with him, it made him appreciate her.

Joe believed Ellen had won a couple of obscure races for women, somewhere, but she didn't look like a race pilot. She just looked like a girl with mouse-blonde hair, and a tongue that could take care of her. He decided that he liked her—he liked her a lot. In a game full of phonies, it seemed to him that she was real, as real as a monkey wrench, only better-looking.

He laid out his wrenches now, and was at work while his exhaust pipe was still all but glowing.

Ellen said: "Justine Pryor was here while you were up. She asked about you, Joe."

"Nice of her."

"She said . . . 'What . . . is that punk cluttering up the place with his power glider again'?"

"I supposed," Joe said, "that it would be something like that."

"Don't you let it worry you. She was on a scout snoop for Frank Manosky, I'll bet anything. It shows they're afraid of you, Joe!"

He answered that with an embittered grunt. He was trying to remember the days when he had admired Justine Pryor with a sort of distant, vacant-eyed awe, like a cow admiring a skyrocket. He had not been alone in that. Justine Pryor may not have been the lightning pilot she was supposed to be, but for the present she was almost a national symbol.

She wore a long, movie-style bob with a sweep to it as if there were head winds in it. Her eyes had a trick slant to them that was plain wicked, and she looked as all girl pilots ought to look. Wherever she went, she was photographed promptly and often, like an accident.

"Sometimes," Ellen Scott said to Joe, "the lady eagle is pretty hard to take."

Joe, his hands already covered with grease, tried to scratch his head with the tip of a little fingernail. Ellen took pity on him, and he held his head down while she scratched it for him. He said: "She let me off easy that time, at that."

"I don't know," Ellen said darkly. "I haven't seen the papers."

"Why the hell doesn't she lay off me?"

"She won't ever," Ellen said, "as long as she's in an official state of romance with Frank Manosky in the newspapers. You make good copy . . . something to wisecrack at. What did you expect, beating her boy by the width of a state, just when they break a quarter-page news photo of Justine kissing Frank good luck?"

"Aw," Joe grumbled, "why can't they forget it?"

"It's a business with Justine," Ellen Scott explained it. "Publicity is more than just a hobby with her. It's a racket, a graft, a living. I'll bet she'll take fifty thousand this year for testimonials alone. Naturally. . . ."

"Well, it isn't a business with me! I just want to fly. I hate this show-off stuff. I'd as soon take a licking as see my name posted in a list, even. I wish I'd never raced at all."

Ellen said: "I can understand that, Joe. That's why I quit racing. I thought I'd like it, but I didn't. I hated it."

"It's my own fault," Joe said. "I ran my neck out. I lost my temper, I guess. But. . . ."

The roar of a neighboring engine swept his voice away. Ellen picked up a clean newspaper the propeller wash had blown in, folded it upon an oily box, and sat on it, hugging her knees.

"Joe, for heaven's sake, why don't you give up all this nonsense? Withdraw your entry, Joe, while you can still get your money back! That thing won't fly three thousand miles. Some days it won't fly three thousand feet."

"It has to," he said.

"You can't fit a forced landing under that thing," she persisted. "Somewhere west of nowhere you'll have to bail out. Joe, you're just throwing away your ship and yourself, too, probably. In heaven's name, why?"

He wanted to answer that. He would have liked to explain to this kind-spirited girl why he had to go on as he did. But he didn't know how. He was thinking about the Border-to-Border, in which he had beaten Frank Manosky. He wanted to forget it, but nobody who had flown in that hard-luck race ever forgot it. Frank Manosky had been expected to win it by such a margin that the race would look like two races. But things went wrong. The racing ships streaked north out of Texas into the teeth of a howler, then blind weather closed over the country, and everything happened to everybody.

Joe Sebring's own memories were lonesome and personal, about the popping of static, like fat frying in his earphones; the inadequacy of his sparse instruments; and the bad light on what dials he had, when the unnatural dusk caught him. Nobody was as surprised as he was to learn he was first home.

Second most surprised was Frank Manosky. Frank had lost his radio beam, and had rummaged around the country for it a long time, getting madder every minute. When he found out that some guy named Joe had come from no place to beat him by a matter of hours, he blew up and issued an ill-considered statement. It had said, in part, that he would undertake to beat this Joe Something ten out of ten, any course, for whatever amount Joe wished to put up. It took a Manosky to get away with a crack like that.

Even with the purse he had won, Joe could not have afforded to put up more than half a dollar, and it curled him. He answered, for publication, that he would gladly show Manosky the way home again in the next national point-to-point. He said he felt sorry for Manosky, wandering around lost like that, and honestly wanted to help him.

Whenever Joe thought about it, his ears burned. He didn't know how to explain to Ellen that he either had to race again, and soon, or crawl under a board.

"I talked myself into a hole," he told her. "I have to fly my way out of it."

"That's crazy! Airplanes fly by means of their engines," she answered him. "You can't fly a mile by the sheer power of hope. What are you going to do when she slings rocker arms all over Missouri? Break out a canoe paddle?"

"What's the matter with this engine?" he demanded weakly.

"It's had five owners at least, and two or three of them are dead. It was a lemon to begin with, and it has more flying hours on it than a ton of owls. And it's going to heat until it melts."

"Maybe," he said doggedly, "it won't, this time."

She was quiet for a few minutes while Joe worked steadily.

"Did you hear about Justine Pryor's new grandstand play?" she said next. "She's going ahead of the race in her flying make-up box that the Hawkwing people furnish her for nothing, and take charge of Manosky's refueling crew at Encampment, just ahead of his last hop."

Joe Sebring made a big show of being fair. "Well, probably somebody needs to take charge of it. Encampment has a kind of a dopey crew, Ellen."

"Yes, it's bad. I know." Then she faltered under a sudden impulse. "Do you want me to fly on ahead and line up a crew there for you? I could be in Encampment some time tomorrow night . . . plenty of time. And I will, if you want me to."

He looked at her oddly, and jumped to the conclusion that it was a gag. "They wouldn't take your picture, toots," he said, "even if you did."

She was silent for so long that he had forgotten all about it by the time she spoke again.

"I think you're the scum of the earth," she said. "I hope Manosky meets you on his way back." And she left there. She was gone as he turned around.

He smiled vaguely, his mind full of engine, and took a few more half-hearted turns of the wrench. Then suddenly he realized what she had offered him, and what he had done. He slung down his wrenches and ran after her. "Hey, Ellen!" It didn't do any good. Her taxi was already pulling out of the parking lot.

Alone in the vast, shadowy hangar, its floor crowded with inter-lapped planes, he felt about the worst he ever had in his life. He would have gone to look for her if he had known where to look. It occurred to him that he knew almost nothing about her at all. He didn't know where she was stopping, or what town she lived in when she was home. But now that she was gone, he was lonely and discouraged, unwilling to work any more, little time as he had left. He didn't care much whether he made the take-off or not.

He began putting away his tools. Then his eye dropped

upon the newspaper Ellen had laid on the box. A face in halftone arrested his glance.

Justine Pryor was beautiful in newsprint again, in helmet and raised goggles. Joe's eye ran down the adjacent interview, and his own name jumped out at him. They had not forgotten to ask Justine about that old joke—the duel between the crack racer, Manosky, and the unknown kid, Joe Sebring, who had beaten him.

It always gave Joe an unpleasant shock to see his name in print. He winced, even before he read the paragraph. *Sebring doesn't figure in this,* Justine Pryor was quoted. *Probably he doesn't even mean to take off. I don't believe you could get him into a race with Frank if you chloroformed him.*

Joe's brow cleared, and he smiled. Meticulously he laid the newspaper back on the box. Then he got out his tools again, and worked until after midnight.

He looked for Ellen all the next day, but she didn't show. It was the eve of the race, and he hardly had time to get to his tuning flights. At noon he took half an hour he could not spare, and went down the hangar line, trying to find out how he could reach her. But the young people had gone to lunch, and he didn't learn anything.

It was starting time, and his ship was warming up on the apron in a murky drizzle before he saw her. She was in a group of people who stood close inside the ropes that held the spectators back. She hadn't come forward to speak to him. The loudspeakers were already roaring his name, warning him to get out on the line, but he went to her, and she walked to his plane with him.

"Look," he said. "I want you to know this. I think you're swell. I think you're great. And you can have anything I've got, any time, ever."

She smiled then, and lifted her face. " 'Bye, Joe." As he kissed her, a flash bulb blazed against the gray day, and Ellen grinned. "I got my picture taken, after all. Good luck, mister!"

Then, presently, he was on the line. The roar of big engines beyond his own, all over the place, blanketed the world with uproar. His hands were sweating, and there was a taut-drawn strain in his left cheek to the point of pain. . . .

He took off muddily, but shook free of the field at last, and the earth fell away, wheeling slowly eastward under him as it fell. Then he got his ship's tail up, and flight relapsed into the alert monotony of cross-country, his eyes flicking through a familiar routine of instruments and horizons.

He had time to think a little bit then, and began thinking about the first time he had seen Ellen Scott. She had made a last-minute entry in a minor trophy race for women, and was trying to get away without her family knowing about it. She didn't have any money with her, and didn't know anybody or any of the ropes, and her tachometer drive had washed out. She was looking like a scared lost kid, who probably ought to be spanked and sent home, when Joe took her under his wing, and got her to the line.

Later, more people knew her name, for she took second to Justine Pryor. She had written to him after that. It had been a nice letter, warm and grateful. Sometimes, he thought, he ought to have answered it.

She was changed a good deal now. She didn't look lost or scared any more—an improvement. She had something, and, now that he was away from her, he realized that it was something he needed.

During the second hour his oil temperature was rising, and it seemed to him that a new note was coming into the voice of his motor. After that he had no time for anything but his worries. By the time he refueled at Kansas City, first of his two refuelings, he knew that he was in all the trouble he had ever expected. He hung his gloves over the temperature indicators, in hopes the ground crew would not recognize what serious shape he was in.

He took off from there in fifth place, and somehow coaxed and cussed his airplane the length of Oklahoma, boring stubbornly into the eye of the sinking sun. He even nursed her over the Continental Divide, mainly by the power of prayer. But it was no good, and he knew it. As the coast ranges began to rise from the desert's rim, he watched his oil pressure flutter weakly, and smelled the engine's incandescent heat, and admitted that Ellen had been right.

By the time he sloped down upon Encampment, he knew that he was lucky even to make the field. He managed to wheel within a few hundred feet of the pumps before he stopped rolling, and a crew ran out to push him in. As he climbed down stiffly, an assistant dispatcher was rattling in his ear: "You're twenty minutes ahead of Tex Campbell, nobody leading you. Frank Manosky is close onto Tex. He's pulled up fast in the last couple of hours. It'll be you and him. If you can hold your pace. . . ."

"Listen," Sebring said. "Listen. I can't. . . ." Then he saw who else was there.

With his mind full of engine failures, Joe had forgotten that Justine Pryor had flown ahead to set up Manosky's crew. She was standing by the pumps, her mouth drawn, her eyes hard. She looked cross.

"Wasn't looking for you out here," she said. "You certainly aren't going to try to go on . . . are you?"

His hand shook as he held the match. "What do you think?"

She must have taken that for a negative, for she looked

relieved. "Tough going, my boy. Better luck next time!"

Joe Sebring bit the cigarette he had been smoking in two, and spat out the pieces. He knew he ought to tell the crew to turn off their pumps and roll his ship out of the way, to make room for other planes that would be going on. But he just walked along the edge of the field by himself, looking at the mountains. They looked dead, ugly, and desolate, with the last of the daylight behind them. When he went back to his plane, he was polishing his goggles.

Justine Pryor was still there, and she was looking dumbfounded. "If you take that thing up, you ought to be grounded for life . . . and I'll see to it!"

"I have to go back and look for Frank," he answered. "I think he's lost again."

The slanted eyes blazed at him greenly. "Smart guy, huh? Well, you remember this . . . I've seen a hundred like you! I've seen them come and go!"

He climbed into the cockpit. "Tell Frank Manosky you just now saw me come and go. Frank will be interested. Prop clear!"

Nobody who heard Joe Sebring's engine at Encampment was surprised that he did not finish ahead of Frank Manosky. As flyer after flyer checked in at Glendale, Sebring was not second. He was not third. He was no place.

Frank Manosky, and some of the other racers, flew back to Encampment to develop a search, as soon as their airplanes were checked over. Within twenty-four hours a number of flyers were gathered there. They got in a few hours' search. Then a nasty stretch of fog and rain came into the mountains, and the search stopped.

Ellen Scott appeared on the evening of the second day. She had started from Encampment by airliner, for her own airplane was in overhaul, and then came on by rail when the liner was grounded by X-weather. She cornered the boss mechanic.

"Harry, I have to have a plane."

"Gosh, Miss Scott, everything's booked. You'll have to. . . ."

"I suppose that's Justine Pryor's plane they're polishing up, over there?"

"Yeah . . . she has a standing order it has to be rolled out and warmed up by daylight. Then, when it's all splattered up, she says . . . 'Roll her back.' "

"Harry, what was the matter with Joe Sebring's engine?"

"Gosh, Miss Scott, plenty. I says to him . . . 'Joe, this kettle is fixing to throw an armful of rods right in your puss.' "

"What did he say?"

"He says . . . 'Jerk them blocks!' It wasn't like Joe."

Ellen went back to town.

It was still dark the next morning, and nobody was around but the radio operator and one mechanic, when the two girls met. Ellen Scott was standing at the teletype in the radio room, running the tape through her fingers, when Justine Pryor came in. Justine's quick step checked a little as she saw Ellen, but for the moment neither girl gave any other sign.

"Miss Pryor," the mechanic said, "your plane is warming on the. . . ."

"Well," Justine snapped, "I can hear it." She turned on Ellen. "Are you flying? Because if you're not, I'd like a look at that tape."

Ellen relinquished it. "I can tell you what's on it."

"I'll see for myself." Justine tossed a newspaper on the

table. "Your picture's on the back page of this one, if you want to admire it."

Ellen didn't. "I don't suppose," she said, "you'd care to put a price on chartering your plane to me?"

Justine Pryor said—"Oh, Lord."—and picked up the tape.

"It isn't as if you were using it yourself. Everybody knows you don't take off in weather like this."

Justine let the tape dangle, and looked at her coolly. "Just what do you think you would do with it?"

"It's going to clear up a little to the west. And I have an instrument ticket. An hour or two west, on Joe's course, I ought to get some visibility. I want to be out there ready to accomplish something. Because the boys have already combed the country close in."

"Forget it," Justine said shortly. "I'll fly that plane when there's flying to be done. You see any chance of getting up out of this, Mac?"

"We'll know a lot more in a couple of hours, Miss Pryor."

"This thing gets me down," Justine fumed. "There are a dozen good pilots here, wasting their valuable time. Before they're through, some of them will have risked their lives and their planes. And why? Because Joe Sebring sold himself the idea he was a smart guy!"

"Justine," Ellen said, "who do you think sent him on?"

"You should know! The whole country has seen that picture of you mugging him at the take-off. If you're going to encourage these short-hour experts to fly 'way out of their class, this sort of thing is bound to happen. They ought to ground you both!"

"Justine, it was you sent Joe Sebring over the mountains in that ruined ship."

"I? I told him not to fly. I all but begged him not to fly!"

"I saw that in the papers," Ellen said. "But I'm no more fooled than you. It burned you up when he beat Frank, because it gummed up your publicity. So you set out to ride Joe Sebring out of the air. You know what you've done. You'd ridden him and taunted him and bedeviled him at every turn. You could do that, because you're a picture-paper flyer."

Justine Pryor appealed to the radioman: "Do I have to stand for this? What right has she to come in here and . . . ?"

"A picture-paper flyer," Ellen said again. "That's all you are, and that's all you ever will be. So you put him in a place where he had to fly, equipped or not. If Joe Sebring is dead, you'll be marked with it all of your life."

Justine Pryor stepped forward and slashed Ellen across the face with her gloves.

"Hey, wait!" the mechanic broke in. "Listen, you dames. . . ."

The radioman said: "Easy now . . . easy. . . ." They got Justine to sit down. In the quiet they could hear Justine's engine, warming futilely in the fog.

"Phony," Ellen said, her voice flat. "As phony as they come. So now the real pilots have to clean up after you." She felt of her lips with her fingers, and studied the lipstick on them. "You can't even read a weather report. If Joe is dead, you killed him."

She walked out then, and, as she passed the table, she tossed her hat upon it, and picked up the helmet that lay there.

They gave Justine Pryor a cigarette, and it seemed to steady her.

"She's nervous," the mechanic said soothingly.

"Look here," Justine demanded, "does she have a plane?"

"No, ma'am! I haven't got any order to let anything out, or warm anything, except your own ship."

Justine was still worrying about a possible publicity scoop. "Then, at least, she can't. . . ."

She stopped. Out on the apron the pulsing undertone rose to a snarling thunder, then definitely pulled away.

"That . . . that's my plane!"

The mechanic looked sheepish. "I guess she must've stole it," he offered.

If Joe Sebring had been near Encampment, they would have found him before the weather closed. He was down on the line of his course, and its checkpoints were bold and obvious. It took no miracle to find him. The only reason Ellen Scott found him, instead of someone else, was that, when she met visibility, she was out there where he was.

Joe Sebring had wrecked an ankle when he bailed out. It wasn't broken; he could hobble on it a little bit. But he had decided he would do better to camp by his cracked ship, where he could easily be found, rather than to attempt a hike.

By the third day he was out of cigarettes, dripping wet, and so hungry he had forgotten what was the matter with him. When a little plane passed over him, flying very high, he went into a brief panic for fear he would not be seen.

He ran limping and stumbling out to a pile of fuel he had, but found it too wet to catch. He tore off his shirt, and waved it frantically. Nobody got any good out of that—it was a khaki shirt, invisible from the air. The searcher apparently saw his crack-up, however, for the plane spiraled downward for a closer look.

Then, with utter amazement, Joe saw that the little ship was approaching to land. Joe Sebring would have sworn that the pilot didn't live who could land a hot ship in that place. The nearest thing to a landing strip was the bottom of a crooked ravine, heavily hazarded with boulders and creosote brush. He held his breath as he watched the accurate triangle, the slow, risky approach. The pilot purposely pancaked with a wallop that not quite washed out the landing gear, tipped up, and bounded upon half-locked brakes—almost, almost recovered to a sensational landing. Then a clump of cat-claw snatched at a wheel, the plane ground-looped, vaulted high off one wing, and crashed in a clump of lodgepole pine.

Yet—she got by with it. Ellen was free of her safety belt and climbing out by the time he got there. He caught her in his arms as she slid down a wing, and carried her, his ankle forgotten, to a place where he could put her down. When he had found she was unhurt, he held her in his arms and shouted at her.

"What do you mean by trying a landing like that? You ought to be grounded a year! Why in hell did you . . . ?"

"Because I'm a plain damned fool, Joe. I saw your cracked ship . . . and I just had to know. Stop talking like Justine!"

After that he just held her and let her cry for a little while.

"I'm the fool," he said at last. "You were right, and I was wrong. You don't know how wrong I was. All my life I've hated to see my name in print. A news camera gives me jitters. And here I've been trying to throw away everything I had . . . and succeeding . . . trying to get something I don't like and don't want. Ellen, I'm glad I didn't beat him."

She pushed away from him a little and stared at him oddly.

"Think I'm nuts?" he asked her.

"No, not exactly. You look pretty tough, with red whiskers, but you're not nuts. But, Joe . . . something has happened to us that you don't know about yet."

He waited.

"It's my fault, partly. . . . Joe, we're suddenly famous."

"Who? You? Me? For what?"

"Do you remember that flash bulb going off when you kissed me, at the take-off? Well, after that, I broke down and told the reporters what you were flying. I said you were racing a patched-up, pretty nearly home-made crate with hardly any engine at all. And they played that up. The picture came out pretty well."

"Oh, my," said Joe.

"Then . . . you were fifth at Kansas City, running very hot, and not reported again. Everybody thought you had probably trailed out of the race. Then suddenly you scorched into Encampment like a bat out of nowhere, way out in front. We all went wild. The newspapers said . . . 'Flying Wreck Blazes Way into Mountains Two States in the Lead,' and all such junk. Then they found out how rotten your engine sounded at Encampment, and everybody was holding his breath for you. Sure enough, you were never reported . . . and that was the most popular sensation of all."

"Popular? But . . . I didn't even finish!"

"Finish? Nuts. Anybody can finish. Getting lost, after all that build-up, was the most sensational thing you could have done. Winning would have been nothing beside it."

Joe said nothing.

"And the search for you . . . special bulletins on national

hookups . . . front page every day . . . you're just a flock of headlines, and I'm not much better off."

"I guess," Joe said, "everything has happened to us."

"That isn't all. That's Justine Pryor's ship. I stole it. I thought I might need help, and there wasn't anybody I could turn to except a couple of reporters. They were crazy about the idea and . . . I was just plain crazy. A couple of them were standing by ready to jerk the blocks, before Justine even had a chance to refuse me charter. Can you imagine what kind of a story they'll make of all that now?"

"No," Joe admitted. "It staggers the mind."

"So now we're both notorious. To all intents and purposes, I'm Justine Pryor and you're Frank Manosky . . . only more so. Everybody wants to give you a job, and give you an engine, and build you a ship. You're rich as hell, and we're both just public property." She began to cry. "But I don't care. I'm so darned relieved."

He thought it over. "Tell me just one thing," he said finally. "Did you bring any grub?"

"Enough for a week. I sneaked it into Justine's ship before. . . ."

"Then," he grinned, "everything's all right. Maybe we can manage to stand prosperity, until it blows over, if we stick together. And maybe"—inspiration lighted his dark-circled eyes—"maybe not until the grub gives out, even!"

She blew her nose, and brightened enough to smile. "That would suit me," she said.

About the Author

Alan LeMay was born in Indianapolis, Indiana, and attended Stetson University in DeLand, Florida, in 1916. Following his military service, he completed his education at the University of Chicago. His short story, "Hullabaloo," appeared the month of his graduation in *Adventure* (6/30/22). He was a prolific contributor to the magazine markets in the mid-1920s. With the story, "Loan of a Gun," LeMay broke into the pages of *Collier's* (2/23/29). During the next decade he wanted nothing more than to be a gentleman rancher, and his income from writing helped support his enthusiasms which included tearing out the peach-tree orchard so he could build a polo field on his ranch outside Santee, California. It was also during this period that he wrote some of his most memorable Western novels, GUNSIGHT TRAIL (1931), WINTER RANGE (1932), CATTLE KINGDOM (1933), and THUNDER IN THE DUST (1934) among them. In the late 1930s he was plunged into debt because of a divorce and turned next to screenwriting, early attaching himself to Cecil B. DeMille's unit at Paramount Pictures. LeMay continued to write original screenplays through the 1940s, and on one occasion even directed the film based on his screenplay.

THE SEARCHERS (1954) is regarded by many as LeMay's masterpiece. It possesses a graphic sense of place; it etches deeply the feats of human endurance that LeMay tended to admire in the American spirit; and it has that characteristic suggestiveness of tremendous depths and untold stories developed in his long apprenticeship writing short stories. A subtext often rides on a snatch of dialogue or flashes in a laconic observation. It was followed by such classic Western novels as THE UNFORGIVEN (1957) and BY DIM AND FLARING LAMPS (1962). PAINTED ROCK, a new collection of short stories and short novels, will be Alan LeMay's next **Five Star Western**.

Additional copyright information: